When
You're
Back

ALSO BY ABBI GLINES

In publication order by series

The Rosemary Beach series
Fallen Too Far
Never Too Far
Forever Too Far
Twisted Perfection
Simple Perfection
Take a Chance
Rush Too Far
One More Chance
You Were Mine
Kiro's Emily (novella)
When I'm Gone

The Sea Breeze series
Breathe
Because of Low
While It Lasts
Just for Now
Sometimes It Lasts
Misbehaving
Bad for You
Hold on Tight

The Vincent Boys series
The Vincent Boys
The Vincent Brothers

The Existence series
Existence
Predestined
Ceaseless

When You're Back

A Rosemary Beach Novel

Abbi Glines

ATRIA PAPERBACK

New York • London • Toronto • Sydney • New Delhi

ATRIA PAPERBACK

Atria Paperback
An Imprint of Simon & Schuster, Inc.
1230 Avenue of the Americas
New York, NY 10020

First Atria Paperback edition June 2015

ATRIA PAPERBACK and colophon are trademarks of Simon & Schuster, Inc.

For information about special discounts for bulk purchases, please contact Simon & Schuster Special Sales at 1-866-506-1949 or business@simonandschuster.com.

The Simon & Schuster Speakers Bureau can bring authors to your live event. For more information or to book an event, contact the Simon & Schuster Speakers Bureau at 1-866-248-3049 or visit our website at www.simonspeakers.com.

Manufactured in the United States of America

10   9   8   7   6   5   4   3   2   1

Library of Congress Cataloging-in-Publication Data is available.

ISBN 978-1-4767-7611-8
ISBN 978-1-4767-7612-5 (ebook)

To Abbi's Army, the world's best street team. I never imagined I'd have a group like this one, supporting my books and being there to lift me up when things get tough. I love you all, and I'm so thankful for each and every one of you.

When You're Back

Reese

It had been twenty-two days, five hours, and thirty minutes since I'd said good-bye to Mase at O'Hare Airport. Once he was sure I was safe at my father's house in Chicago with my newfound family, he returned to Texas to his family's ranch, which just couldn't run without him.

Going back with him had been so tempting. I was ready to start my life with Mase, and I was anxious to make his home our home. But first, I needed to do this.

A little more than a month ago, a polished, well-groomed Italian man had shown on my doorstep in Rosemary Beach, where I had worked as a maid for some of the town's wealthiest families. Not too long after I'd met Mase, the father I had never known—and hadn't even been sure was alive—had walked back into my life, wanting to be a part of it.

Mase had been right there with me, holding my hand through it all. Benedetto had stayed with us in Rosemary Beach for a week, and then we'd all flown to Chicago together.

I soon found out that not only did I have a father, but I also had a brother. He was two years younger than I and a total riot; Raul made me laugh constantly. I also had a grandmother, or nonna, as she preferred to be called. She loved to sit and talk with me for hours. She told me stories about my father when he was younger and showed me pictures from Raul's childhood. She also told me how she'd pleaded with Benedetto to find me. He had his reasons for not coming after me. That was all he ever told anyone. I wanted to hate him for not coming for me when I was younger, but I couldn't. My life had led me to Mase.

The time I'd spent with them had been wonderful, but I had missed Mase. Talking to him every night wasn't enough. I needed him. I needed him more than I needed a father, brother, and nonna. Mase was my family. The first person who had ever truly been there for me after a lifetime of abuse from my mother and stepfather.

Now, finally, I was home—or in the place that had been about to become my home before my father had shown up. Mase and I were planning to move in together, but that hadn't fully happened yet.

I hadn't let Mase know I was coming back early. I wanted to surprise him.

The cab driver pulled up outside of Mase's parents' house on their sprawling ranch. A quick look at the dark house told me no one was home. Good. My surprise was just for Mase. I quickly paid the driver, pulled my one piece of luggage out of the trunk, and hurried toward the stables. Mase's truck was parked outside beside another truck I didn't recognize.

I propped my suitcase beside his truck, then made my way down the small hill to the stables. I knew he'd be there, since he'd told me he wasn't planning to train a horse that day. My heart was racing with excitement, and my hands itched to touch him. I was thankful I'd had time with my family, but I wasn't leaving Mase again. If he couldn't go with me to Chicago next time, then I wouldn't go. They'd all just have to come visit me here.

Female laughter drifted from the stables as I got closer. Was he handling a business deal? I didn't want to interrupt him if this was a client. I couldn't throw myself into his arms if he was in the middle of dealing with a horse and its owner. I paused outside the stables.

"No, Mase, you promised me the other night that we'd go riding today. You can't take that back now for work. I want my ride," the woman said. Her voice sent a chill down my spine. It was young and flirty; she was too familiar with him.

"I know I promised, but I have work to do. You'll have to be patient," he replied.

"I'm going to bat my eyelashes and pout if I don't get my way," the female threatened.

"No games today, Aida. I seriously have stuff to do. You've been monopolizing all of my time the past two days," he said in a voice that had me backing up. I knew that voice. He used it with me.

"But I'm bored, and you always entertain me," she argued playfully.

"Seriously, I need you to give me some time to get things done today. I'll entertain you tonight. We'll go out, get something to eat. I'll even take you dancing."

My heart cracked. What I was hearing couldn't be interpreted many ways. Mase was spending time with another woman. He cared for her. I could hear it in his voice.

I had assumed he was cheating on me once before. I didn't want to do that again, but what else could this mean? I glanced at the truck parked beside his and then back at the door leading inside. My heart wanted me to run away and curl up in a ball to keep from falling apart.

But my head was telling me I needed to face this. Whatever it was. I should at least give Mase the chance to explain before I left.

All the excitement I had been feeling moments earlier completely died. I was filled with emotions I couldn't even begin to untangle.

The woman's laughter floated outside, followed by Mase's low chuckle, which always made me feel warm inside. He was enjoying himself. Being with this woman made him happy. Had I been gone for too long? Had he needed someone else?

Or had he figured out that I wasn't as special as he thought I was?

"Hello. Can I help you?" the female voice asked.

I snapped my head up to see her standing in the doorway of the stables as if she were about to leave. She was tall, with long blond hair pulled up in a ponytail. Without any makeup on, she was still stunning. Full lips and perfect white teeth. Her large green eyes seemed to glitter with happiness. Mase had that effect on women.

"Are you here about a horse?" she asked, when I said nothing, just stood and stared at her. The jeans she was wearing were tight and showcased slender hips and tiny thighs. She was model-thin. I was not.

"I-I, uh—" I stammered. How could I talk to this woman? I should have just left. Confronting Mase while she stood there, looking like a Barbie doll, was going to be impossible. He would look at the two of us standing side by side and see who was the better pick.

"Are you lost?" she asked.

Yes. I was completely lost. Everything I thought I knew was true, everything I thought was mine, wasn't. "Maybe," I whispered, then shook my head. "No. I came to see—"

"Reese!" Mase's voice boomed from behind the woman, and before I could say anything else, he was pushing past her and wrapping me up in his arms. "You're here! Why didn't you tell me you were coming home? I would've come to get you. God, you smell good. I missed this. I missed you so fucking much!"

I stared over his shoulder at the woman, who was no longer smiling. She was staring at me as if I were repulsive.

"I wanted . . . I wanted to sur-surprise you," I tripped over my words, not sure what to think. I had heard him with her. I knew he was spending time with her, and she obviously didn't want me here.

He grabbed my face and covered my mouth with his. As unsure as I was and as hurt as I had been by what I'd heard between him and this woman, I quickly pushed my feelings to the side. The taste of Mase and the feel of his lips moving against mine always undid me. He feasted on my mouth, and I clung to him as I inhaled his scent. The flick of his tongue over mine made me shiver. Nothing else in the world mattered when I was with him like this.

"*Ahem.* I'm still here, guys. Remember me?" The other woman's voice broke through my delicious haze, and I froze. Pulling back from me, Mase actually chuckled and glanced back at the woman, keeping his arms tightly wrapped around me.

"Sorry, Aida, my woman is home, and I'm going to be all kinds of tied up for at least the next forty-eight hours. Maybe more. Go find something to do back at the house," he said, then kissed the tip of my nose as he turned his back on the woman again.

"Kinda rude running off and leaving me and not introducing me to your friend," she replied, with obvious distaste in her tone.

Mase grinned down at me and winked. "She's a diva. You'll get used to her." Then he turned his head toward the other woman. "Aida, this is Reese, the woman I haven't shut up about. The one I talk to for hours every night." He turned his attention back to me. "Reese, meet my only girl cousin, Aida. She's a bit spoiled, a lot dramatic, and easily bored."

Cousin? If that's all she was, why was she glaring at me like I was standing in her way?

I looked back at Aida, and she smirked. Although I was comforted by the knowledge that they were related, something about the way she looked at me felt like a challenge.

How . . . odd.

Mase

Having Reese in my arms again helped ease the frustration that she hadn't let me know she was coming home. I would have picked her up from the airport. I didn't like the idea of her arriving with no one to welcome her.

"Did you take a cab?" I asked, not liking the idea of that, either.

She nodded but didn't say more.

"I wish you'd called me." I pulled her against me and walked her back toward my truck. I was tucking her inside and getting her to our home. Where she belonged.

"I thought surprising you would be fun." She seemed off, like she was upset. Maybe she was just tired from traveling.

"I'd say call me next time, but there won't be a next time. I'm not going to be separated from you like that again. If you want to go to Chicago, I'll go with you."

Her body seemed to relax then as she leaned closer to me. This was what I needed today. Aida was exhausting and demanding. Having her here had helped ease the hurt of missing Reese but only because she was full of distracting, nonstop chatter.

As soon as Momma got home she would have to entertain Aida.

I took Reese's suitcase and put it in the back of my truck, then slid a hand under her perfect ass and lifted her in. The giggle that escaped from her sent a warm sensation rushing through my veins. I needed her laughter.

"I'm not letting you leave my side for at least two days. I'm needy," I said as I climbed in. "Besides, I picked you up a couple of books at the library last week. I'm ready for you to read them to me."

She laid her head on my shoulder and sighed contentedly. "I read to you almost every night while I was gone."

"Yeah, but you weren't naked in my bed."

She laughed again, making everything in my life feel perfect. She was what I had been waiting for. Everything before her had been dull, including the girls. No one had made me feel the excitement of waking up every morning and seeing her face. Or going to bed every night with her in my arms.

"You want me to read naked in bed?" she asked in an amused tone.

"Hell, yeah, I do. I want you to do everything naked."

Reese tilted her head back and looked up at me. "You're not serious."

I glanced down at her smiling face. "Yes, baby. When I'm talking about you being naked, I'm very, *very* serious."

She laughed again and I pulled her closer to me. This was what I needed.

Reese headed inside as I lifted her suitcase out of the back. I took a moment to watch her walking into my house, soon to be our house. It felt different with her here. She brought warmth and sunshine with her.

Glancing back over her shoulder, she smiled. "Are you coming?"

"I was just enjoying the view," I replied with a grin, and I made my way to join her.

As soon as I was through the door, I set her suitcase down and reached for her. She squealed in surprise as I picked her up and carried her over to the sofa. Sinking down onto the worn leather, I held her in my lap as she clung to my shoulders.

"Welcome home," I said, just before I captured her lips with mine.

The guy in me wanted to strip her naked and fuck her against the door. But the man who knew what she needed was going to hold her and love her a little while first. I never wanted to make her think it was all about sex for me. I had been in love with her before we'd ever had sex. She was too precious to be treated like a hot piece of ass . . . although her ass *was* divine.

Reese took my hat off and tossed it onto the seat beside us, then sank her fingers into my hair. Her kisses were like warm honey, and I was pretty damn sure I could just do this forever. Soft curves in my hands and the mouth of an angel were more than I had ever imagined. *Reese* was more than I had ever imagined.

The soft plumpness of her lips brushed against my bristly chin as she trailed kisses over my face. "You haven't shaved," she whispered.

"I wasn't expecting you."

"I like it. It's sexy," she murmured, and her mouth came back to mine.

"It'll hurt your soft skin," I replied, before taking her kiss deeper and drowning myself in the sweetness. My hands slid under her shirt to touch her heated skin, and she shivered in my arms.

"I think I'd like it to hurt a little. If it's you that's doing it," she said, shifting in my lap until she was straddling me. Her dark hair fell around her shoulders as she gave me a shy, sexy little smile that made my blood pump harder.

I reached up and cupped her face and brushed my thumbs across her cheeks. "I could never hurt this skin. That would be tragic."

She blushed and leaned forward, pressing her face into my hands. "I need you," she whispered. The spark of excitement in her eyes was all I needed.

"Lift your arms up." She didn't question me but did exactly as I said. I took her shirt off carefully and placed it beside us. Taking in the sight of her in a bra made me feel like a teenager again, seeing tits for the first time. Fuck, I'd missed those.

"I want them in my mouth, but I need to shave," I told her, unable to stop soaking in the sight of them.

"Please, Mase. I want to feel your scruff on my skin. I love it. I really do."

She was going to drive me crazy. I wanted to see the marks of me on her skin, too. I felt guilty wanting to hurt her in any way, but hearing her beg for it was too tough to ignore.

I reached behind her and unclasped her bra. My heart

thudded in my chest as both full breasts fell free. Those perfect pebbled nipples needed me as much as I needed them.

Fuck it. I bent my head and pulled one into my mouth, letting it roll over my tongue. Reese's sighs and moans as she pulled tightly at my hair sent my adrenaline spiking. I wanted to bite down and hear her scream in pleasure. But I couldn't. I never wanted to scare her or hurt her. I wanted her always to feel safe and cherished in my arms.

"I want your shirt off," she said with a soft moan.

I'd do whatever she wanted. I let her nipple pop from my mouth and jerked my shirt off in record time. My mouth was back where it wanted to be in seconds. Reese's nails gently trailed down my chest, and her palms covered my pecs as she bent her back and whispered my name in a way that made me feel like a king.

Once she'd been scared of this. Knowing she trusted me to love her and make her feel good was something I'd never take for granted. She had been broken once, and I intended to make sure she never felt that way again. I would protect her from all harm. With me, she would always know she was safe.

Her hips began to rock, and I bit back a wince. My dick was about to burst out of my jeans. Having the zipper press even harder against it caused pain along with the pleasure.

I let her nipple go in order to claim her mouth again and inhaled her sweetness. When she whimpered, I broke the kiss and touched my forehead to hers. "Let's take off your jeans," I said, wanting to touch more of her.

"Let's take off *yours*," she replied with a grin, then eased back off me and stood up.

I watched as she unzipped her jeans and slowly began to

wiggle out of them. I was entranced. A pair of black satin panties came into view, and the pain from the zipper got worse. I
reached for my own jeans and unfastened them to give myself
some relief. But I never took my eyes off Reese. She slid her
jeans down her legs and tossed them aside.

"Panties," I said, but it sounded more like a growl.

Her face flushed and her eyes lit with desire as she quickly
removed those, too. I had her completely naked now. I wanted
her like that in my arms for fucking ever.

"You haven't taken off your jeans," she said, staring down
at my boxers which were now in view.

"I was working on it. You distracted me."

"Then stand up and let me help," she replied, grinning
wickedly.

I swear I'd jump off a cliff if she asked me to. That grin
could make me do anything.

Reese

Mase stood up, and my eyes went to his rippled stomach, which was so hard I couldn't keep my hands off of it.

"Anything you want," he said, looking at me like I was his world. This was the Mase I knew. The man I trusted. The man I knew would never hurt me. I felt guilty for doubting him earlier. I hadn't had any safe and secure relationships until recently, so I didn't understand how to trust in them. Until now.

I closed the little space between us and tugged on his already loosened jeans until I realized he was still wearing his boots. I loved his boots. "You need to take those off," I reminded him.

He smirked, bent down, and pulled them both off with ease. "Done."

He made me feel as if I could ask him anything and he would do it. That was a powerful yet humbling emotion. I continued pulling his jeans down, pausing to appreciate his muscular thighs and perfect calves.

I stood up, glancing at his boxers. My cheeks felt warm as I touched them and gently began pulling them down. I could hear Mase's breathing hitch, and that sent a shiver of anticipation through me. My being close to him like this—especially

13

his penis—excited him. That was a powerful feeling for me, too. Knowing he liked it when I took my time, I paused and glanced up at him when I had the boxers low enough to expose him. His eyes were heated with excitement.

Leaning in, I pressed a kiss to the swollen red tip.

"Fuck, baby," he groaned.

I liked that. No, I *loved* that.

I continued moving his boxers down his legs, then stood up and touched his stomach as I ran my hands up his chest. His hands settled on my hips.

"Let me take you to bed," he said, pulling me flush up against him.

"OK," I whispered.

He picked me up and held me closely to his chest as he walked me to his room, my legs wrapped around his waist. His mouth covered mine in a hungry kiss before he laid me down gently on the king-size bed.

I stared up at him, letting my legs fall open as I held my hands up for him. I wanted him covering me. Completing me.

Mase fell into my arms immediately.

"I love you," he said fervently as he kissed my neck. "I love you so much I can't breathe. You are my heart, Reese. My life." He continued to kiss a trail down my neck until he was nibbling at my collarbone.

"Mase," I moaned, lifting my hips. I wanted more. I wanted him inside me. Filling me.

He slipped a hand between my legs, and his finger slid inside. "So fucking wet. Damn," he groaned. He took that same finger, slipped it into his mouth, and sucked on it before lowering himself until I felt the tip of his hardness press against me.

This was what I needed. This connection.

He slowly sank into me, stretching me with his size. The muscles in his arms bulged, and he closed his eyes tightly. I watched his beautiful face. The tight clenching of his jaw and the vein in his neck. All of it made me hum with pleasure.

When he was finally deep inside me, his eyes opened, and he met my gaze. There was so much emotion in them that I felt my own eyes start to tear up. He didn't have to tell me how he felt about me—I could see it. He bared it all to me in that moment, and I knew it.

"Wrap your legs around me," he said in a hoarse whisper as he lowered himself even further. His mouth brushed my ear.

I did as I was told.

"So good," he said, whispering his praise.

I held on to his shoulders, ready for him to move inside me. I knew it would be so incredible—more than incredible, really; there was no way to describe how I felt during sex with Mase.

"Keep those legs open wide, baby. Let me love you until you can't remember your name."

With those words, he nearly brought me to the brink of an orgasm. Was that even possible?

"Sweet, just like that. Let me make you feel good. I want you to reach heaven the way I do when I'm buried inside you."

I started to assure him I was there, that I knew what he was feeling, but his hips rocked, and I lost all thoughts and the ability to breathe as I held on tight. He made growling sounds of pleasure as he sent sparks of heat through me.

When the first orgasm crashed over me, he scooped me against his chest and whispered how beautiful I was and other sweet things I couldn't quite remember—his words and the steady rhythm of his movements were already bringing me to my next orgasm. Quickly. I held him close, clinging to him for dear life.

By the time the third one hit me, Mase roared and cried out my name as his body shook with his own orgasm. He pressed his face into my neck as he gasped for air.

Feeling him fall apart over me made me tremble with pleasure once more, before we collapsed together, our hearts thudding wildly.

The sound of knocking broke into my dreams as I forced my eyes open. I looked around in the darkness of the room, Mase's warm body pressed against mine as I lay wrapped in his arms. After the third time we'd made love last night, we had both passed out.

Mase groaned and blinked his eyes open. "What the . . . ?" his sleepy voice asked.

"Mase!" a woman's voice called out. I recognized it. Aida was here. "Open up. I brought food."

"Shit," he growled as he eased out of bed. He walked over to the closet and grabbed a pair of jeans and a T-shirt. When he turned back to me, he gave me a pleased grin. "You hungry?"

I was sleepy but hungry, too. It looked like we had slept past dinner. I nodded.

"I'll get your suitcase. Take your time getting dressed. I'll fix your plate," he said, bending down to press a kiss to my lips.

Mase left the room. I lay there, tucked into blankets that smelled like him.

I could hear Aida at the front door as her voice filled the house. "What took you so long? I brought you food. I'd think you'd be more grateful."

"Thanks," he said flatly.

"Where you going?"

"Bringing Reese her suitcase," he replied as his footsteps made their way back to the bedroom.

"Jesus, Mase. You could've at least picked up her underwear before you let me in," Aida said in an annoyed tone. She didn't like me. I wasn't just imagining that.

He didn't respond. When he opened the door, he rolled his eyes and grinned at me. Our discarded clothing was tucked under one of his arms as he carried my suitcase with the other hand. "Ignore her."

He tossed our clothing onto a chair and winked at me. "Get dressed and come eat."

When he walked out this time, I sat up, worried about how to face Aida.

I didn't want his cousin to dislike me, but I wasn't sure if I had any control over that.

Mase

Momma had sent over enough food to feed an army. I reached to get two plates out of the cabinet. "Tell Momma I said thanks for this. Reese is probably starving."

Aida was standing on the other side of the counter with her hand on her hip. "You only got two plates. Is Reese not eating with us?"

Us? Shit.

Aida wasn't leaving. It wasn't that I didn't enjoy hanging out with her when she visited, but I didn't want her hanging out with us right now. I just got Reese back. I wasn't ready to share her yet.

"Uh, I figured you had already eaten."

She looked hurt. "No, I wanted to eat with you. We always eat dinner together."

Damn. This wasn't going to be easy.

I saw movement from across the living room and glanced up to see Reese standing there in a pair of cutoff sweats and a T-shirt that hugged her body just right. I wanted to be alone with her, but Aida was here, and I couldn't hurt her feelings.

I smiled at Reese. "Come eat. I'm getting you a plate ready now." She glanced at Aida then back at me nervously.

"She can't fix her own plate?" Aida asked in a snarky voice I didn't like.

"Yeah, she can. But she doesn't have to. Not when I'm here."

My reply seemed to annoy Aida, but she didn't say anything else. What was her deal? No wonder Reese looked nervous. Aida wasn't being her usual bubbly self. Reese was seeing a bad side of her.

"I don't mind. I can do it," Reese said as she moved toward me. She seemed eager to please. This was the Reese I'd met. The one who was unsure of herself and shy. Aida wasn't going to bring that out of her again—I wouldn't allow it.

"I got this, baby," I assured her.

She walked toward the cabinets. "I'll fix the drinks, then. Aida, what would you like?" she asked.

I looked over at Aida, who seemed even more annoyed before she saw me looking at her. Then she smiled. "I'd like sweet tea, please," she replied. Her smile didn't meet her eyes. I was going to have a talk with Aida. Something was off with her.

"Momma sent tea, too," I told Reese, sliding the gallon of tea across the counter to her. "I'll take some, too."

Reese smiled up at me, relieved about something, and began pouring three glasses. "I love your momma's sweet tea," she said.

And my momma loved Reese. I was surprised she hadn't brought the food over and had sent Aida instead.

I slid a plate over to Aida before I picked up Reese's and walked over to the table to set it down. Reese was setting the glasses of tea at each seat. I pulled her to me and kissed her.

"Eat a lot. You need your energy," I whispered in her ear, then walked back over to fix my own plate.

Aida was frowning at me. "Do you have to do that with me here?"

"My house, Aida. I can do what I want in it. You don't like it, you can eat at Momma's." I was tired of her snarky attitude. She was never like this. I didn't know what had gotten into her.

"That's rude," she said, sounding hurt.

"When I want to kiss Reese, I will. Get over it."

I didn't wait for her to say more but grabbed several pieces of fried chicken and a biscuit before walking back to the table.

Reese was sitting there, staring down at her plate with her hands in her lap, looking a little lost. "You're not eating," I said.

She lifted her gaze to meet mine. "I was waiting for the both of you to join me."

Aida sat down on the other side of me. "So are we still going to the cattle auction tomorrow? I've been looking forward to that all week."

I kept my gaze on Reese. "Doubt it. I don't expect Reese will want to get up that early."

"Reese doesn't have to go," Aida replied.

She was really starting to piss me off. "She just got home. I'm not going anywhere without her."

I felt Reese's soft hand touch my arm. "If you need to go to the cattle auction, I can get up early. Don't let me be the reason you don't do things you need to do."

She was trying hard to fix things. I didn't want her thinking she had to do that. This was her home. She belonged here.

"My need to have you all to myself is what's keeping me from doing things. I don't intend to do shit tomorrow. I want you alone in this house with me."

Reese blushed, and a smile tugged at her lips before she lowered her gaze back to the plate in front of her.

"Does that mean you aren't going to the Stouts' for the barbecue tomorrow night? They're expecting you."

The Stouts owned one of the two biggest ranches in a fifty-mile radius; my family owned the other. I'd grown up with their son, Hawkins. We weren't close friends, but we both knew we'd be taking over our fathers' positions one day.

I glanced at Reese. "You up for a Texas barbecue?"

She nodded. "That sounds fun."

Having Reese on my arm and introducing her to the people in town made going to the barbecue feel more bearable.

"Guess I lost my date. Who will I dance with now?" Aida asked with a pout.

She was being exasperating. I had started to respond to her ridiculous comment when she dropped her fork to her plate with a clatter and stood up.

"You don't want me here. I'm just in the way." She turned and headed for the door.

What the fuck? Where had my fun little cousin gone? She'd turned into an angry crybaby. This was not like her at all. "I need to talk to her," I told Reese. "I don't know what's gotten into her."

Reese nodded and gave me a smile that didn't meet her eyes. That bothered me. I had to fix this thing with Aida so she would stop upsetting Reese.

I followed after Aida only to find her at her truck, crying. "What is wrong with you?" I asked as I walked down the steps toward her.

She looked up at me with a tear-streaked face. "I don't . . . she's . . . you don't have any time for me with her here."

"Aida, this isn't a competition for my time. My life and my future all belong to Reese. She's a part of me. We are a package deal. I would think you'd be happy for me, but you've hardly even spoken to Reese. I want you to be friends. You're my family, and she will be, too, soon enough."

Aida wiped at her tears and sniffed. "So we won't ever get to do anything together again, just you and me?"

I tried to understand why she was crying. I had always given Aida all of my attention when she visited. She didn't come over often when we were growing up, but when she did, I treated her the way I treated my little sister, Harlow. But things had changed, and we were adults now. She wasn't that little girl anymore. I didn't have to let her follow me around, and I wasn't obligated to entertain her every second she was here.

"If you would give Reese a chance, I know you'd love her. She's easy to love. Everyone who meets her loves her. We can all do things together. I'm not cutting you out of my life, but you have to understand Reese *is* my life now."

Aida sniffled and sighed. "You won't have time for me anymore."

She was right. I wasn't going to be able to drop everything and escort her everywhere she wanted me to. "We're grown-up, Aida. We aren't kids anymore. I'm not a single guy who has time to do whatever you want. Those days are gone."

She nodded, and her tears seemed to dry up. "OK. I can accept that. But can you at least not ignore me?"

"I don't ignore you."

Aida seemed appeased by that and started to open her truck door. I reached around her and opened it for her. She climbed inside. "Be nice to Reese next time, will ya?" I said, before I closed her door and headed back inside to my girl.

Reese

I finished eating alone and cleaned up my plate and Aida's before walking back to the bedroom. I wasn't sure how long he would be gone, and I wished I could shut my mind off about what was going on. I had only just met Mase's immediate family. How would it affect us if his cousin hated me? Because I was pretty sure she did, though I wasn't sure how to fix that. Harlow was so sweet and accepting of me, and she was his sister. It should be easier to win over his cousin.

The stream of warm water felt wonderful when I stepped into the shower. Just as I closed the door, I heard Mase call my name.

I had started to open the door and answer him when he appeared in the bathroom doorway. He walked straight toward me, and I watched him through the glass as his eyes trailed over me like I was his meal instead of the food I'd left for him on the table.

He opened the shower door, and our eyes met just before he started stripping off his clothes.

"I left your food on the table for you," I said, watching him step out of his jeans and boxers.

"Can't eat knowing you're naked and wet in my shower," he replied, and stepped under the stream of water with me.

"You didn't eat very much." I sounded breathless.

He smirked. "Turn around, Reese. Put your hands on the wall. I want to kiss my spot."

His spot was the freckle under my left butt cheek. He was obsessed with it. And when he wanted to be naughty, that was the first thing he kissed.

My body trembled with the thrill of what was to come, and I turned and leaned toward the wall, bracing myself as I lifted my bottom up for him.

His finger brushed back and forth over the freckle. "Love this. Drives me fucking crazy," he said, and his lips pressed against the small of my back and began trailing kisses over my ass until he was licking and kissing the freckle. "My freckle," he said against my skin.

My knees felt weak, and my body trembled.

"Spread your legs," he demanded, and the tone of his voice made my insides quiver. I moved them apart and hoped I wouldn't crumple to the ground.

"My pussy," he said, just before his tongue began tasting me there.

I was his. Everything about me belonged to Mase Colt Manning. I cried out his name as he began to tease my clit.

"Be good, baby. This is my dessert."

"Mase," I whimpered, not sure I could stand there much longer.

"Yes, baby?" His warm breath bathed my sensitive flesh, and the pulsing need grew stronger.

"I can't . . . stand," I said, feeling my knees start to give out.

His hands were on my waist, picking me up and turning me around. "I got you," he said, before bending down, taking one of my legs, and draping it over his shoulder.

Another whimper escaped from me at the sight of Mase on his knees like that.

"Just let me love you," he said with a fierce look, before burying his face between my legs.

I grabbed his shoulders and cried out as he took me to another realm of pleasure.

My eyes fluttered open as my back hit the soft bed. I glanced up at Mase. His body was dry, but his hair was still damp. The smug smile on his face made me ache for more, even though I wasn't sure I could *do* more.

He pulled back the covers and crawled in beside me, then covered us both up.

"Glad you're back," he said, holding me close. "That must have been one hell of an orgasm."

I frowned. "It was . . . but . . ." I couldn't remember what had happened after it hit me. I had splintered off into a million pieces, and Mase had just kept sliding his tongue over me until I couldn't take any more. I'd been begging and gasping for air and then . . . nothing.

"Either you're exhausted, or I'm just that damn good," he said, sounding pleased with himself.

"What happened?" I finally asked.

Mase bent his head and kissed my forehead. "You passed out from your orgasm after screaming my name. It was amazing."

"Oh, my God," I whispered. "I didn't know that could happen."

"Me, neither," he replied, still grinning.

"You just kept going and . . ."

"You taste like a fucking cinnamon bun, and when you come, it's like sweet cream. I couldn't stop. It was too damn good."

I buried my face in his chest. I was embarrassed and pleased.

He chuckled and held me tighter. "Told you that pussy was gonna own me."

I inhaled him and clung closer.

"Sleep, baby. You're exhausted. Get some rest."

"I love you," I said, leaning my head back to look up at him.

"And that makes me the luckiest man in the world."

His eyes warmed me up, inside and out. I laid my head against his chest, and sleep came quickly.

Mase

The next day, I discovered that Aida and I would be the only Colts at the Stouts' party. My stepdad had needed to drive to Austin for business, and my momma had gone with him. She had called and asked me to take Aida with us. She didn't want her to drive over there alone. I wasn't sure I trusted Aida to be nice to Reese yet, but I'd asked her to come with us anyway.

After making love to Reese on the kitchen table after breakfast, then again on the sofa while we were supposed to be watching a movie, and then again on the bed when she'd gone to take a nap, she'd really needed to get some rest. I'd woken her up an hour ago so she'd have time to get ready.

I heard a knock on the door, and when I opened it, Aida smiled up at me. She was wearing a red dress that probably cost too much money and a pair of stiletto heels, which actually wasn't unusual for this kind of party. The Stouts were incredibly wealthy and ran in elite circles. She seemed happy and in a better mood. Relieved, I stepped back and let her in.

"Reese should be ready in a few minutes," I told her.

Just as I said the words, the bedroom door opened, and I turned to see Reese stepping out of the room wearing a short blue-jeans skirt with a pair of boots. All I saw was her legs.

Holy hell, her legs were really out there. *Mine.* Men weren't going to be able to take their eyes off them.

I lifted my gaze to see she was also wearing a pretty white blouse tied around her waist. The fabric showed off the sun-kissed glow of her skin. I met her gaze, and my breath hitched. Her long dark hair was pulled to the side and draped over one shoulder. As always, her makeup was minimal. I wouldn't be able to let her out of my sight tonight.

"You're gorgeous, baby. Maybe we should just stay here," I said, honestly considering it.

Reese's smile brightened, and a smile tugged at the corners of her lips.

"Uh, yeah . . . I guess blue jeans will do," Aida said hesitantly.

Reese's face fell immediately, and worry touched her brow. I knew her wardrobe was limited. She didn't have designer clothing like the other women who would be at this barbecue, but no one there would hold a candle to Reese. An expensive dress couldn't compete with her.

"I thought it was a barbecue. I can find something dressier. I didn't know—"

"You're perfect. So perfect I'm not leaving your side all night," I told her.

She glanced from Aida to me, still looking unsure of herself.

"He's right. You'll do. We need to go, or we'll be more than just fashionably late," Aida said at my side.

I walked over to Reese and pulled her to me. "You're breathtaking. I swear." I slid my hand to rest on her lower back and led her to the door.

Aida forced a smile and turned to leave.

"She looks so nice. I should find something dressier. I do have heels," Reese said.

"No. She's overdressed," I assured her.

Reese didn't relax, like she wasn't sure she believed me.

Aida went to the passenger side of my truck and opened the door to climb in first. I paused for a moment, then led Reese to my side and helped her climb into the cab so she could sit in the middle seat beside me. I didn't want to hurt Aida's feelings by asking her to get out and let Reese in first. I climbed up behind Reese and settled in.

"I won't be able to reach the radio," Aida said, clearly annoyed. I didn't think she had intentionally meant to sit between Reese and me, but I wasn't sure.

"Good," I replied. I never liked it when Aida controlled the radio.

Once I had us headed toward the main road, I slipped my hand over Reese's bare thigh and squeezed. That small gesture seemed to ease her some.

"Who will be at this party? Just the people in town?" Reese asked.

"Everyone the Stouts do business with. Bankers, lawyers, ranchers, and then the folks from their restaurant chain who own one of their franchises. They fly in from everywhere," Aida said, sounding pleased with herself.

Reese stiffened again.

"You make the Stouts sound more important than they are," I said to Aida, shooting her an annoyed glance.

Aida shrugged. "They are to those of us whose fathers aren't legendary rock stars."

"My father is a rancher," I replied, not liking the fact that she'd brought up Kiro. I didn't talk about my biological father much. He wasn't a part of my life; my stepdad was the one who had actually raised me. My only connection to Kiro was through Harlow. He had been a much bigger presence in my half sister's life.

"Whatever, Mase. You have fame in your blood. Get over it," Aida said, and smirked at me.

Reese smoothed her skirt nervously. She was worried about this damn barbecue now. I wanted to forget the stupid thing. I didn't want to force her to do anything that upset her.

"We can go home now. You just say the word," I told her, squeezing her thigh again.

"What? No, we can't! I'm not missing this party." Aida's high-pitched whine was out of line.

"I want to go," Reese said, and leaned into me.

"If you decide you want to go home at any point, just tell me. I'll get Aida a ride." I ignored the glare Aida was shooting my way.

Reese didn't say anything; she just leaned in even closer to my side.

The large iron gates stood open, and a couple of large men in suits stood at the entrance. I stopped and rolled down the window.

"Name?" The man asked.

"Mase Colt," I replied, leaving the Manning off of my name. Most people around here thought of me as a Colt.

He nodded. "Welcome, Mr. Colt. You may proceed."

I followed the extravagant brick drive until we came up to the front of the three-story house, which was bigger than most folks' homes around here. The valet stood waiting, but I wasn't letting some kid in a tux park my truck.

When the valet approached, he had a fake smile plastered on his face.

"I can park my own truck," I informed him.

He looked confused. "Uh, well, it's out there . . . but it's a walk." He pointed out toward the left of the house, where several cars were already parked.

"Thanks," I replied, then glanced back at Reese and Aida. "Y'all can go ahead and get out here so you don't have to walk."

Reese reached up and took my arm. "I'll stay with you. I don't mind walking."

Aida rolled her eyes and reached for her door. "I'm getting out."

The valet hurried to open her door the rest of the way and helped her out. As soon as he closed it, I drove down to the parking area. I never liked leaving my keys with some stranger. A man could park his own damn wheels.

Reese

The backyard where the barbecue was being held looked like something out of a magazine. Lanterns hung from massive oak trees, casting their light as nightfall approached, and twinkly white lights were strung from tree to tree, making a whimsical canopy over the tables and white upholstered chairs, which didn't look like they belonged outside.

A band was on the stage playing everything from popular country music to classical. There was even a dance floor, with the same canopy of lights as the eating area.

But what stood out the most was the way the women were dressed. Aida had been right—a blue-jeans skirt didn't fit in here. Not even men were wearing blue jeans. I should have questioned the fact that Mase had on a pair of straight-legged khakis with his boots instead of his usual jeans. The button-down baby-blue Oxford shirt was dressier than anything he ever wore. Why hadn't I insisted that he let me go back and change?

His hand rested on my lower back as he directed me toward the crowd. People stood around in groups, champagne glasses in their hands, as they talked among themselves. Diamonds glittered on the women's hands, wrists, ears, and necks. Had

Mase never been to one of these "barbecues" before? I figured he'd come to many of them. Why had he said Aida was over-dressed?

"Mase Colt," a tall, broad-shouldered man with graying hair at his temples called out in a deep voice as we stepped into the light. "It's good to see you. I wasn't here for the last exchange. Hawkins said everything went smoothly, as always."

"Yes, sir. Dad was pleased," Mase replied.

This was the second time he'd been referred to as Colt, not Colt Manning, tonight. I'd never heard him drop his last name before.

The man's attention moved to me, and for a moment, I wanted to run and hide under a table. "And I see you've brought a beautiful woman."

Mase's hand remained on my back. "Yes, sir. This is Reese Ellis. Reese, this is Arthur Stout, a business partner of ours and the host of this 'modest' barbecue."

Arthur chuckled. "That's actually my wife's fault. She can't do anything small. It's a pleasure to meet you, Reese. About time Mase had a woman on his arm. Every good man needs a good woman at his side. Been trying to tell Hawkins that for years, but he doesn't listen."

"When he meets her, you won't have to tell him anything. It'll just happen," Mase said, making my heart thud and my chest feel warm.

Arthur Stout grinned and nodded his head. "Reckon that's so. God knows that's how it was with his momma. God rest her soul, she took a part of me when she left this world."

"Arthur, honey, you must meet Chantel. She's from the club. I was just telling you about our lovely tea the other day," said a woman who looked only a few years older than me. The diamond on her hand caught the light and twinkled.

"Coming, darling," he replied. "I must go. You two enjoy yourselves."

I watched him go, then looked up at Mase, a little confused.

"Piper is his second wife. His first wife passed away ten years ago from cancer. He married Piper four years ago," Mase said, understanding my confusion.

"But she looks so young," I whispered, watching the woman cling to the arm of a man who had to be in his sixties.

"She was twenty-two when he married her. His son, Hawkins, is a year older than her."

Ew.

Mase looked at my face and chuckled. "Come on. Let's get a drink. Stout started his own brewery about seven years ago. He has some ciders you might like; I know you're not a fan of beer."

I walked with him toward the extravagant bar.

"There you are! I saw Aida earlier, and she said you were here. I wondered if you dropped her off and then went to hide."

Mase stopped and turned his head toward the voice, just as I did. An attractive guy with short blond hair and pale blue eyes was walking toward us.

"Aida didn't tell me you brought a date," the man said as he stopped in front of us, looking at me with a pleased smile.

"Hawkins," Mase replied, with a harder tone than he'd used with Hawkins's father.

Hawkins grinned even bigger and finally looked at Mase. "Please tell me she's another cousin," he said.

Mase's hand slid around my back, now gripping me at my hip as he pulled me toward him. "No. She's mine."

Hawkins kept smiling.

"Reese, this is Hawkins Stout. Hawkins, this is Reese Ellis," Mase said, sounding annoyed.

Hawkins held out his hand. "It's nice to meet you, Reese Ellis," he said.

I slipped my hand into his, wondering if we were going to shake, but he lifted my hand to his mouth and pressed a kiss there. I froze. I wasn't expecting that.

Mase cleared his throat, and Hawkins's gaze left me to look at Mase with amusement. "Easy. I understand," he said with a smirk, then took a step back. "Enjoy your evening. We have several new brews you would enjoy."

"Headed to the bar now," Mase replied.

Hawkins gave me one last smile before excusing himself to greet other guests.

I started to say something but decided against it. Mase didn't say anything, so I took his lead and walked toward the bar.

He ordered a beer, and I decided on the blueberry cider after trying a sample. Once we had our drinks, we turned to see Aida coming directly for us . . . or for Mase. She looked upset. Really upset.

"I need you," she choked out.

"What's wrong?" he asked

She looked pointedly at me and then back at him, pleadingly. "I can't talk about it here. Please," she begged.

Mase nodded. "OK, where do you want to go?"

"Somewhere we can be alone. I just . . . I can't." She covered her mouth and squeezed her eyes together dramatically. I wasn't sure if I believed something was wrong.

Mase nodded toward the house. "Let's go inside."

She nodded, and then Mase's hand was at my back, guiding me forward. I knew this wasn't Aida's idea of "alone." I had started to say something when she saw I was following along.

Her face crumpled again. "I can't talk about this with her. Just you."

Mase shook his head, as if he was about to argue.

"It's Heath. He's here with *her*," Aida said with a sob.

Mase's frown grew. "I know that's hard, Aida, but I can't leave Reese alone. She doesn't know anyone here."

This was my chance to win Aida over, if only a little. "Yes, you can. I have a drink, and I can sit in one of those lovely chairs and wait. Go with her. She's upset."

Mase didn't seem convinced.

Aida sobbed again. "Please, Mase. I need you to talk me off a ledge."

"Go," I repeated.

Finally, Mase sighed and pressed a kiss to my forehead. "I'll be back quickly," he whispered.

I nodded, and he followed Aida inside. I watched them until they reached the house, and then I turned to survey the scene. I was at a party full of strangers, and no one else was sitting down yet. Maybe the tables were off limits until we ate.

I made my way to the shadows, where the lights from the trees didn't reach. I could see the house from here, and when Mase returned, I'd be able to see him.

It wasn't until I was out of the light and my eyes adjusted to the darkness that I saw I wasn't alone. I paused. Should I be concerned? Or maybe I should just excuse myself and find another dark spot.

"He leaves you for another woman, and you hide in the dark," a deep voice said. I could just make out the shape of a man leaning against a bale of hay with a beer in his hand. I studied him quickly to see if I should be worried. The first thing I noticed was his jeans, then his white Oxford shirt, similar to Mase's blue one. But his sleeves were rolled up to his elbows. The only thing I could make out clearly from his features was his green eyes, which burned with an inner light.

"You decided yet?" the man asked, making me self-conscious that I was still staring at him.

"What?" I asked, confused.

A low rumble that sounded like a laugh came from him. He tilted his head, and I realized his hair was pulled back in a ponytail. Although it was dark, I could make out highlights in his hair. Seemed like he spent a lot of time in the sun. "Am I safe to be around? That's what you're trying to decide, isn't it?"

Was he safe to be around?

"That's debatable, if you ask me," he said.

"What's debatable?" I asked.

He took a drink of his beer and studied me a moment before responding to my question. "Whether I'm safe or not." He laughed again, although it was low and almost hard to hear. "You have an expressive face."

How could he even see my face out here in the dark?

He shifted his stance and crossed his left ankle over his right one. I glanced at his boots and realized they weren't like Mase's boots. They were more like combat boots.

"Why are you out here in the dark?" I asked, not meaning to actually say that out loud.

He held up his beer. "Drinking my beer in peace."

I nodded. That made sense. Maybe he didn't like crowds, either.

"Why are *you* out here in the dark?" he asked.

I glanced back at the house, and there was no sign of Mase yet. "I . . . my boyfriend went to deal with something. His cousin is upset."

The guy stared at me while he drank his beer. It made me nervous. It was like he could read all my thoughts. "But he knows you aren't comfortable in a crowd of people you don't know. A man shouldn't leave his woman."

He didn't understand the situation. Who was he to judge something he didn't know? "His cousin is upset. I told him to go."

"Doesn't change the fact that he shouldn't have left you."

I didn't like this man. I would rather face the crowd than hide out here with him. "Don't make assumptions about something you know nothing about," I said angrily, before turning and walking back into the light, just in time to see Mase, his eyes scanning the tables for me. His long strides quickened as he walked down the steps and passed several people who were trying to speak to him. When his gaze finally landed on me, he looked relieved.

I hurried toward him, deciding I wouldn't mention the guy in the shadows.

Mase

Aida was being dramatic. She'd started dating Heath when she came to visit us last year, but it had meant more to her than to him. She'd broken up with him a year ago because he'd cheated on her with a former friend of hers. I had warned her when she started dating Hawkins's cousin that Heath Stout was a player. Now, a year later, she was having a dramatic breakdown? She knew he'd be here.

I hated leaving Reese, but I knew Aida wasn't going to let up until I did. I scanned the crowd for Reese. She wasn't where she'd said she would be. I heard my name called by several people, but I kept my focus as I searched for her. When I turned and saw her walking toward me, I let out a sigh of relief. She was OK.

"I'm sorry about that," I said, as I slipped my hand back around her waist and pulled her against me. "Aida was being a drama queen."

"It was fine. I didn't mind at all. I just walked around and checked things out."

I glanced back to where she had come from and saw a man walking out of the shadows. He was staring at me with an amused smirk, but I didn't recognize him. He was dressed in jeans and combat boots and had a more impressive ponytail than I did when I pulled my hair back.

"River, come here, I want you to meet someone," Arthur Stout bellowed. I turned my head to see Arthur walking up to me as he waved at the man with the ponytail.

River didn't seem to be in a hurry.

Once he reached us, Arthur slapped him on the back. "Mase, meet River Kipling. He's been running the Stout and Hawkins Steakhouse in Key West. He added fresh seafood to the menu, and it's now our most successful franchise location. I've brought him here to do the same for the Dallas location. He knows his seafood," Arthur explained. "River, this is Mase Colt. He's our main supplier of beef cattle, other than the ones we raise ourselves. Colt ranch is about pure quality. You need to make a visit and see what he's got going on there."

"From Key West to Dallas. That's a big change of scenery," I said, not liking the way his gaze kept going to Reese or the way she tensed up beside me.

"Some scenery is better than others," he replied, his eyes fixed on Reese. I didn't like that shit at all.

"Expect River to come for a visit with me next week. I've got a few other people I need to introduce him to. Drink up, and take that pretty girl out on the dance floor," Arthur said, before he turned to River and led him away. River took one more look at Reese and followed him.

"I don't like him," Reese said firmly.

I glanced down at her. "Who?"

"That River guy. He rubs me the wrong way."

Grinning, I leaned down and kissed her lips. I wanted those

lips. I also wanted her up against a wall with her short little skirt pushed up around her waist. The boots could stay on.

"I'm not a fan, either."

Two hours later, I had forced a smile and spoken to everyone my stepdad would have wanted me to. Reese had been safely tucked at my side the whole time. I'd had to remind myself not to get furious when men's gazes fell to her legs. She was showing them off tonight, and I had to expect that. But I didn't have to fucking like it.

Reese had surprised me and chosen the ribs for dinner. I was positive she was the only woman eating ribs. Watching her eat a rib was sexy as hell, and I'd had a hard time focusing on my own plate of food; my eyes kept going to her mouth and the way her tongue kept flicking out to lick the sauce off her lips.

I was ready to head home and looked around for Aida. I wanted to leave her here so I wouldn't have to deal with her wanting to come back to my place tonight to visit. I had plans for Reese and that skirt . . . and those boots.

"Dance with me," Aida said, and her hand clasped my arm. She had snuck up behind me.

"I'm ready to go," I replied.

She pouted. "You haven't danced with me all night. We always dance at these parties."

I had started to say no again when Reese stepped slightly away from me. "Go, dance. I'll wait right here."

"See? She doesn't care. Let's dance." Aida was in a much better mood than the one I'd left her in. She was a little too happy. Her mood swings the past two days were giving me whiplash. I wasn't used to having her around for this long;

she usually only came for a few days a couple of times a year, though she did stay for a while with us last summer.

I didn't want to dance with her. I hadn't even danced with Reese, mostly because I was afraid she would panic at the idea of dancing with all these people here. It was obvious she didn't feel comfortable among strangers. Dancing with Aida seemed wrong.

"Please, please, please," Aida begged, drawing attention to herself as she pulled on my hand, trying to tug me forward. "We can leave after one dance."

We would leave as soon as I was ready.

"Go," Reese said, pushing me gently.

Dammit. I didn't want to do this. Aida and I had been taught to dance by my mother when we were kids, and it had entertained Aida when she was younger. She hadn't liked doing things I enjoyed, like fishing, hiking, and camping. Harlow had loved doing all those things with me. But Aida was always different. She enjoyed attention.

She kept pleading and pulling my arm. I wasn't getting out of this.

"Fine. One dance," I replied, and she beamed brightly.

I glanced back at Reese as she pulled me forward. "I'll be right back."

Reese nodded and smiled at me.

This was a bad idea.

Reese

"Does he always dance with his cousin like that?" a deep voice asked. Although I had only met the guy once—or twice, technically—I knew who it was without looking.

"Yes," I replied, even though I had no idea.

They really were something. I had no idea Mase could dance like that. People had stopped talking and were watching them now. One dance had turned into two.

"He's not real smart," River Kipling said with a drawl.

There he went again, making me mad. I turned to glare up at him. In the light, he was much more attractive than I had realized. There was a carefree look about him, and he seemed unaffected by the party around us. "He's brilliant," I replied.

River grinned and shook his head. "You're something else, Reese Ellis."

I wasn't sure what he meant by that, but I didn't care. He said mean things about Mase. I didn't like him. At all. "They like to dance," I said, feeling the need to defend Mase even more.

"Then he should have danced with you. Shame to have you on his arm and miss the chance to spin you around the dance floor."

Mase hadn't asked me to dance. I thought maybe he didn't like to, but he was putting on a show with Aida. I watched as he picked her up and did some flippy thing. The crowd clapped and cheered. "She's better at dancing than I am," I admitted. "I couldn't do that kind of stuff."

I thought that would shut up River Kipling, but I was wrong. "That looks like work, not fun. Holding a woman close and feeling your body brush against hers, the tease of knowing you can't touch anything the way you want to." He paused. "That's why you dance."

I wanted him to shut up. I didn't need him in my ear. I was trying to find a way to fit into Mase's world. This guy wasn't helping by putting doubts in my head. The song ended, and Mase shook his head when Aida obviously begged him to dance one more time.

When he turned toward me, I saw him tense up as his gaze shifted to River beside me.

"Bet he stops dancing now. You're welcome," River said in an amused tone.

I glanced back at him as he walked off. He did fill out a pair of jeans well, and he had a swagger when he walked. But he was infuriating otherwise.

"Was he bothering you?" Mase asked, as his hands slipped around me.

I forgot the aggravating man and looked up at Mase. "No, he was just talking about how good y'all danced."

Mase frowned at that. "Yeah, sorry she made me do two. She's coming now, so we can go."

I nodded.

Aida's laughter trailed behind us as we walked toward the

truck. "I love dancing!" she squealed loudly into the darkness. "We need to do that more."

Mase didn't respond. He walked me toward the driver's-side door and opened it, then lifted me up and set me on the seat, as if I couldn't do it myself.

"I can do that without help, you know," I teased.

He leaned in. "But if you do it, your skirt will ride up, and I'll see my freckle. Aida's with us, so I wouldn't be able to take a lick."

My face grew warm, and I shivered, thinking of how good it felt when he did that. "Oh," I managed to reply breathlessly.

"Yeah, *oh*," he repeated. "When we walk through that door tonight, I'm bending you over so I can visit my spot."

Anticipation made my breath hitch. "M'kay," I said, not knowing how else to respond to that.

"We need to go out dancing next weekend," Aida said as she opened the passenger door and climbed in.

Mase moved me over and climbed in beside me.

"Reese can come and watch. We can dance all night," Aida said.

I wasn't going to watch Mase and Aida dance all night, but I didn't say anything.

"Glad you enjoyed it, Aida," Mase said simply.

"I loved it! No one else dances as good as you," Aida said. Then I felt her gaze on me. I turned toward her and saw a smirk on her face. "I guess Reese doesn't know how to dance, since you didn't dance with her all night."

That stung. A little.

Mase's hand slid over my thigh. "She can dance."

"Oh . . . well, then, you must not enjoy dancing with her.

It's OK, Reese. He's had me to dance with for most of our lives, and we move together like a well-oiled machine."

I didn't like the way she said that. There was something off about her tone.

"I love dancing with Reese. Let this go, Aida."

That still didn't answer my doubt. I was beginning to think maybe Aida was right. He didn't want to dance with me because he was used to showing off, and I couldn't show off with him.

Mase let Aida out at his mother's house with a "good night," and I knew that was his way of letting her know she wasn't welcome up at the house with us. I started thinking about what he'd said about bending me over, and I squirmed a little in my seat.

"I didn't ask you to dance tonight because I was afraid you wouldn't want to in front of all those people. You seemed nervous, and I didn't want to add to that. But there is nothing in the world I'd rather do than hold you against me."

He had waited until Aida was gone to explain, and I appreciated it. I didn't want her to know I had felt intimidated by them dancing. Leaning over, I kissed his arm. "You're right. I would have been nervous."

"Feeling your body move against mine is the ultimate turn-on. If I'd danced with you, I wouldn't have been able to stay. We might not have made it to the truck before I had my hand up the back of your skirt to cup your luscious ass."

This time, I laughed. I liked that excuse; it made me feel much better. "Why don't we go inside, and you can show me exactly what you want me to do? I remember it had something to do with me bending over . . ."

Mase's eyes lit up with hunger as he grabbed me and pulled me out of the truck. "Not sure I can make it inside," he said, just before his mouth was on mine. I held on to both his arms and sank into him. His kisses always made me weak in the knees. Nothing else in the world mattered when his mouth moved over mine. He made everything perfect by simply kissing me.

I let out a small cry of protest when he broke the kiss, but his eyes gleamed with excitement and possessiveness.

"Bend over, and hold on to the seat," he said, in an authoritative tone that made my stomach feel fluttery.

"Out here?" I asked.

He gave me a wicked grin. "No one's out here, and it's just a little play, baby. I swear."

That look on his face could make me do anything. I turned around and did exactly as he said.

"Fuck," he muttered, as his hands slid up the backs of my thighs until he was pushing my skirt up and over my bottom and I was exposed. His finger ran over my freckle. I couldn't see it, but I knew where it was. He spent a lot of time there. It was also currently a little sensitive from his lack of shaving last night.

"I don't like you in short skirts," he said. "Makes me worry that you'll bend over and someone else will see this. It's mine. I don't want anyone else seeing it."

I closed my eyes and took a deep breath. He was going to kill me with his very sexy words before he even did anything.

"Spread them wider," he demanded.

His hands took hold of my thighs and pushed them open until I knew I was completely exposed to him. I let out a whimper as his finger slowly traced the heat between my legs.

"So wet," he whispered, then pressed a kiss to my inner thigh. "So soft."

"Oh, God," I moaned, feeling my legs tremble.

"I'm not God, baby," he said, sounding amused. I grinned and held on to the seat in front of me. "But I'm about to take us both to heaven." I heard his zipper slide down.

He was going to make love to me out here. Out in the open.

"I know I said I was gonna just play, but you're soaking wet and smell like sweet cream. I need inside of you." His voice was deep but gentle.

His hands grabbed my waist, and he slowly sank into me as I moaned his name. Being filled with Mase was incredible. I yearned for this feeling all the time. Every time he gave me that sexy smirk or I saw his muscles flex under his T-shirt, I daydreamed about his muscular arms holding himself over me, flexing as he pumped in and out of me.

One of his rough hands caressed my bottom. "Love this," he groaned.

I couldn't agree more. The only thing I loved more than this was the man himself.

Mase

Over the next week, I got very little work done on the ranch. When I wasn't spending every second I could with Reese, there was Aida, who always seemed to need me for one thing or another. Because Reese had insisted I go, I took Aida horseback riding to her favorite spot down by the lake. Then, on another day, Aida had wanted to go to the cattle auction with me. Although I had intended to take Reese, she had said she would rather stay at the house and read so I should take Aida.

I knew Reese was trying her best to get Aida to like her. It was why she was constantly pushing me to do things with my demanding cousin. I just wasn't sure Aida was appreciating it the way she should. Every chance she got, she complained about Reese or the time I spent with her. I was growing weary of defending Reese all the time to her. Aida was going to have to change her attitude about Reese, or I wasn't letting her near Reese again.

If Aida thought this was a competition, she needed to know she had already lost. Aida was my cousin. She had been competitive with Harlow one time when her visit overlapped with Aida's. Giving Harlow all my attention hadn't gone over well with Aida then, either. But we'd been kids, and I had simply ignored her. We were adults now, and she was acting insane.

My biggest concern was that Reese was going to get bored being at the ranch all the time, so when I got the call from Harlow to invite us to Lila Kate's first birthday party in four days, I was relieved to have an excuse to escape with Reese. It was past time Aida went home.

Blaire and Rush Finlay were hosting Lila Kate's party at their backyard pool, and since their house was practically on the beach, Harlow was doing a luau theme. I hadn't even realized I'd been an uncle for a year already. The time had flown by.

Reese was excited about going back to Rosemary Beach, which only worried me more. She had nothing to do here in Texas. When I wasn't with her, she was alone. I hated the idea of her being lonely or sad. I had to fix this. Maybe get her back into classes and encourage her to keep working on her GED.

Although I preferred not to rely on my father—the biological one, that is—my sister wasn't always so cooperative. Slacker Demon's private jet was scheduled to pick us up and take us to Florida in a couple of days. Our father's rock band still went on huge tours all the time, so the private plane was a necessity for them. Not for me. I could argue with Harlow, but I knew she'd end up winning. The jet was already stopping in Dallas to pick up a guest of Blaire and Rush's so she wanted Reese and me to take advantage of it.

I got things tied up and taken care of so that Reese and I could fly out the day before the party. We were also planning to spend a few extra days in town afterward; I knew Reese wanted to see her friend Jimmy. He had been her closest friend, and she spoke with him at least once a week on the phone.

When we landed in Florida, Harlow had a silver Mercedes waiting for us at the airport for me to drive the rest of the way into town. I knew this had to be our father's doing, but it was more for Harlow than for me. Harlow was the only one of Kiro's three kids—including me and Harlow's half sister, Nan—he'd had a hand in raising, so Harlow actually thought of him as a dad. He loved her the most, but then again, she was easy to love. Hell, I had loved her the most, too, until Reese walked into my life. The only person who was ever bitter about this favoritism was Nan.

Reese touched the butter-colored leather interior of the Mercedes and smiled. "Wow. This car is something," she said in awe. She had been in awe all day. The jet had made her jaw drop for a good five minutes. Just watching her walk around and explore the cabin with childlike wonder had made the experience worth it, even if it was courtesy of Kiro.

"I'm sure this is from Kiro, too," I explained. "If I'd been paying for this, we would've been driving a Dodge truck."

"W-will, uh, will *he* be there? At the party?" she asked, almost with caution. As if asking would upset me.

I nodded. "He wouldn't miss his granddaughter's birthday for the world. At least, any granddaughter Harlow gives him. And this will be the only one. Harlow can't have any more kids. She almost died giving birth to Lila Kate."

"So Harlow is his favorite?"

I laughed. That was an understatement. "Harlow is the only child his beloved wife, Emily, gave to him. He adored Emily. He still does, even though she suffered brain damage in an accident years ago and can't speak or do anything on her own."

Reese frowned. "What about Nan?"

I sighed. "We didn't even know Nan was our sister until a few years ago. Kiro didn't claim her, and her mother lied about who her father was. It was a clusterfuck. And Nan is a mean viper. You know that. You've dealt with her. She hates Harlow because our father loves her. It's not a good family situation."

"That's sad," Reese said simply.

I glanced over at her. "What's sad?"

She looked up at me with eyes full of sorrow. "To be told your father was someone he wasn't and finding out the father you do have doesn't want you. That would make anyone unhappy. Then to see that father adore another daughter while he barely acknowledges you. That has to cut deep. I imagine she has suffered from a lot of emotional wounds in life."

Was she really making excuses for Nan? No one had an excuse for being evil and cruel. Yet here Reese was, feeling sorry for her, even after working as Nan's housemaid for a short time and experiencing her ugliness firsthand. Reese was being understanding of why Nan was the way she was.

"You might change your mind after you've spent more time with her. If that ever happens."

"Won't she be at the party?"

I doubted it. "Before Grant met Harlow, he had a thing with Nan. When Grant fell in love with Harlow, that didn't help Nan's hatred for her. The fact that Nan donated blood to Harlow when she was giving birth to Lila Kate made a huge difference and at least showed a little humanity. But I doubt that's enough for Grant to invite her to his daughter's birthday. Besides, Kiro and Nan don't get along. Every time they're in the same room, it usually ends in screaming."

Reese didn't ask me anything else, but I could tell her

wheels were turning. She was trying to put this all together so that it made sense. Problem was, nothing with this side of my family made sense. Kiro had fucked it all up years ago. Harlow and her daughter were all I cared about on this side of my family. And Grant, at times. He'd proven worthy of my sister, but I was still watching him. I'd kill him if he ever hurt her.

Reese

I had cleaned fabulous houses before, but none of them compared to this one. The Finlays' place was massive and gorgeous. It sat directly on the water, and expensive cars filled the driveway. We were staying with Grant and Harlow, but they had left early to get things ready. We had offered to keep Lila Kate, but Grant said she'd get fussy if he wasn't close by. Mase said it was more likely that Grant would get fussy. Watching Grant Carter with his daughter, as she wobbled around, trying to walk, was adorable. He hovered over her constantly, ready to catch her if she fell at any moment. The few times she did fall, he reacted lightning-fast, swooping her up and checking her out while kissing her little chubby knees.

"Kiro's here. He must have Dean with him, since they brought the limo," Mase said without emotion.

I was going to meet two of the music industry's legends, but Mase was unimpressed. Then again, if Kiro had ignored him most of his life, I understood why he wasn't excited about seeing the man. I wasn't sure I was going to like him, anyway. He had a lot counting against him in my eyes.

Before I could step out of the Mercedes, Mase was there

to give me a hand and help me down. I let him help me, since I was holding the large pink-and-brown polka-dot box with Lila Kate's birthday present in it. We had gone shopping in Dallas to find the perfect present for his niece's first birthday. When we saw a pair of pink cowboy boots with a matching pink leather hat, Mase had insisted we buy both of them. They were perfect gifts for Lila Kate from her uncle Mase.

I had bought her a plush horse that she could carry around to go with her new outfit. Mase had said that he would teach her to ride one day, but after watching Grant with his daughter, I doubted Lila Kate would ever get on the back of a horse. I didn't think Grant could handle that.

"Let's go party," Mase said with a wink.

I smoothed out my yellow sundress after he took the present from my hands. It was a luau, so I had dressed in my best beach dress and a pair of strappy sandals. Harlow had been dressed similarly, so I wasn't worried about being underdressed for this party.

"There are a lot of people here," I said, looking around at the cars that kept arriving.

"Yeah, Grant's been in Rosemary Beach most of his life. He's friends with everyone."

Mase knocked once, and a woman who could have been a Victoria's Secret Angel opened the door, smiling brightly. "Mase, hello," she said, then turned her striking green eyes to me. "Hi, Reese. How have you been?"

"Thank you for having me, Blaire. It's wonderful to see you again."

Blaire stood back and waved us in. "Me, you, Harlow, Bethy, and Della need to have a girl day soon. Even if we need to fly to Texas to do it," Blaire said, sounding determined.

I had never had a girl day. That sounded like fun.

"Harlow is out at the pool. Grant has Lila Kate in the pool with Rush and Nate. Y'all go on out there and see everyone. I'm on door duty right now. I'll take the gift and put it with the others."

"Thanks, Blaire," Mase said, then placed a hand on my lower back to lead me through the Finlays' breathtaking home toward an impressive back patio, with stairs that led down to a pool that looked like it belonged at a luxury resort.

There were people everywhere. Some of the women were in bikinis, while others were dressed in short sundresses like mine. The men who wore swim trunks all looked like fitness models. I scanned the crowd, looking for a familiar face other than Harlow's.

My eyes landed on someone I hadn't expected to see here. Lounging in a chair in a pair of swim trunks, showing off a tan that most of the other men didn't have, he looked like he lived on a boat. His hair was exactly as I remembered it from the barbecue. Brown with highlights, pulled back in a messy ponytail that looked like he hadn't brushed it. Even with aviators on, I could feel his gaze locked on me. What the heck was he doing here?

"Mase, it's so good to see you," a female voice said from behind us, and I turned to see a face I recognized. I'd met

Della Kerrington before, but this time, she was holding a small bundle in a blue blanket.

"And Reese," she said. Her genuine smile made me feel immediately comfortable around her. "I'm so glad you're here."

Mase nodded his head at the baby in her arms. "Congratulations. I heard the little guy was born last month."

Della gazed down at the bundle and smiled. "Yes. He came a month early, but he's perfect, and I can't remember ever being this happy. He completes us."

"What's his name?" Mase asked.

"Cruz," she said, looking back up at us. "Cruz Woods Kerrington."

"Cool name. I like it," Mase replied.

"Me, too. And congratulations," I added.

Della smiled warmly. "Thank you both. I intend to spend a little more time with you, Reese. But right now, I have a hungry little boy to feed," she said before heading inside.

"I like her," I said as I watched her go.

"Yeah, she's the best thing that ever happened to Kerrington. Dude was a man-whore before her," Mase said, and winked at me.

I laughed as he slid his hand around my waist and led me down the steps and toward the pool. I glanced over at the chair where I'd seen that familiar face earlier, but he was gone. Weird.

"Watch me jump, Daddy!" a small voice called out, and I turned to see an adorable little boy standing on the top of a rock waterfall. He looked too small to be up there, but he had a determined gleam in his eyes.

"I'm watching. Show me what you got," a man called out from the water. I was too worried about the little boy to take my eyes off him and see who his daddy was. Did the boy's mother know he was up there?

The boy flashed a big grin that told me he was a charmer, even if he was just a little kid. Then he jumped high and tucked his small body tightly and flipped twice in the air before diving into the water.

Everyone clapped and hollered, including me. I was amazed.

His little head surfaced, and he had pride shining on his face. It was precious. "Told ya I could do two," he said, looking at Grant. Then he swam over and gave a muscular, tattooed man a high-five. Without Rush Finlay turning around, I knew exactly who it was. I'd seen him in magazines and on television before. He was Dean Finlay's son. He turned around to smirk at Grant, who was chuckling.

"Don't doubt my boy," he said, which only made Grant shake his head as he laughed.

Rush Finlay had turned to swim toward the ladder when his eyes lifted and saw Mase. If I weren't completely in love with Mase, I'd have to say this man was the most beautiful thing I'd ever seen. But I did love Mase, and no one compared. Rush would have to come in a close second.

"Mase," Rush said with a smirk before pulling himself out of the water. I had to look away, because, seriously, he was pushing it. He even got out of the water in an attractive way.

"Talented kid you got there," Mase replied.

"Hell, yeah, he is. Just like his daddy," Rush said.

"And he likes to remind everyone of that," Grant called out from the pool.

I forced myself to turn back around to face a wet Rush Finlay. I was thankful he had a towel wrapped around him now. Didn't take away from the water droplets running down his chest, though.

Rush turned his attention to me. "Reese," he said, surprising me by knowing my name. "Nice to meet you."

I managed to get out a "Nice to meet you, too."

Then he turned his attention back to Mase. "You seen Kiro?" Rush asked.

Mase shook his head. "Not yet."

"He's inside with Emily. He doesn't want her out in the sun too much."

Mase's eyes went wide. "Emily is here?"

Rush ran a hand through his short, wet hair and nodded. "Yeah. He didn't want her to miss her granddaughter's birthday."

Wow. From everything Mase had told me about Harlow's mom, I never would have guessed Kiro would take her out of the special medical facility in Los Angeles, even for a day.

"Guess now that the world knows she's alive, he feels safe taking her places," Mase said, with a concerned look in his eyes.

"Dad says he thinks this is the last year Kiro will even record with Slacker Demon. He's afraid Kiro is ready to leave the band. I figure it's time for all of them. They've been at it for twenty-five years, after all."

"It's about time they retired," Mase agreed.

"Music world won't agree, though," Rush said. "But if

they're all ready, then it's time to stop. I just don't know if my dad is there yet."

They continued to talk, and I turned my attention to the others. I scanned the pool and a cabana set up nearby, and my eyes collided with those aviators again. He was still watching me.

Mase

We hadn't seen Harlow since we arrived at the party, but now we knew she must be with her parents. Being around Emily was hard on her. She'd lived most of her life thinking her mother was dead. When she had discovered Emily was very much alive but unable to communicate or do anything, it had been difficult for her to handle. Had Kiro even thought about Harlow's feelings when he chose to bring Emily here?

Frustrated, I looked for someone I could trust with Reese so I could find my sister and make sure she was OK. If our father had ruined this day for her, I was going to be pissed. For once, he needed to think of someone other than himself.

Blaire stepped outside, and I touched Reese's elbow. "I need to check on Harlow and make sure she's OK with her mother being here. It's all new to her, and I'm worried. I'm going to leave you with Blaire for a few minutes. Is that OK?"

Reese nodded. "Of course."

Blaire saw us headed her way and walked toward us. "I was going to go inside and check on Harlow. She's not out here, and I know Emily is here, so . . ." I trailed off, knowing Blaire would understand my concern.

Blaire nodded. "Go on in. This gives me time to get to know Reese. We'll have Mai Tais and chat."

I glanced at Reese, and she nudged me to go. "She's giving me Mai Tais. I'll be fine. Go."

Once it felt safe to leave her, I walked toward the house in search of my sister.

It didn't take long to find her. She was standing in the kitchen, staring blankly at the wall. This was what I'd been afraid of. Harlow shouldn't have to deal with this shit on her daughter's birthday. Sure, it was her mother, but she hadn't been given long to process that she even had a mother, much less accept the fact that our father had kept her locked away and a secret from everyone.

"Harlow," I said quietly, not wanting to startle her.

She turned around, and her eyes were watery with unshed tears. "Hey," she said softly.

"I'm going to tell him to leave. He shouldn't have done this to you," I said, my voice betraying my anger.

She shook her head. "No, that's not it. He told me he was bringing her. It's just . . . I'm not crying because of her. I'm crying because of him. Watching him with her is heartbreaking, Mase. You haven't seen it. There's this side to our father that I didn't even know existed until recently. When you see him with her, it makes complete sense. *He* makes complete sense. She was his everything, and he lost her so tragically after such a short time. I just see him, and I think . . . what if I hadn't made it? What if I had died in that delivery room?

What if Grant had been left to raise Lila Kate without me? Would he have been able to be this adoring, wonderful daddy that's he's turned out to be, or would he have become what Kiro became?" She sniffled and wiped at her eyes. "You hold so much against him, and I understand why. I know he didn't do right by you or your mother. But he was so broken, and for a moment, my mother saved him, only for him to lose her. He doesn't know how to be happy. He lost the love of his life."

I started to argue that the son of a bitch had kids to think of and responsibilities, but I stopped, because Reese's face flashed before me. I'd found her. She had changed my world, and even after such a short time, I knew she was my future. What if I lost her? What if tomorrow she was gone? How would I cope? Could I ever heal from that?

"How is he with her?" I asked, needing to believe that Kiro could love like that. Even still, I wanted the man who gave me life to have some redeeming qualities. I'd grown up believing he had none.

Harlow smiled, and her eyes showed so much emotion. "He treats her like she's precious. The most important, most precious thing in the world. He brushes her hair and tells her stories of their past. He calls her his angel. It's . . . it's beautiful. I wish he'd had a chance to live life with her. I think we'd both have grown up with a very different kind of father. Maybe even Nan would be different because of it."

Could loving someone destroy you that completely? I'd never thought so deeply about it, but more than once, I'd wondered if Kiro had a soul. I watched the way he lived and wondered how my mother could have made such a massive mistake sleeping with that man even once.

But if he'd lost his soul when he'd lost his future with Emily, then it made him less of a monster in my eyes. It made him human—not the rock god the world knew but a man who had loved with his entire being and lost that love.

"He loves us. He loves you. He's proud of you. I heard him telling Emily . . . my mom . . . about you the other day. Apparently, my mother loved you, too. He was telling her what a fine young man you've turned into and how proud she'd be of the little boy she had adored. He doesn't show emotion well, but Emily is his heart. She's his only link to happiness. I want her here with him."

I'd never had Kiro tell me he was proud of me. I swallowed the emotion that tightened my throat and nodded. "OK. Then come outside with me. Enjoy your daughter's party. Let's celebrate life. Yours and hers."

Harlow grinned and walked over to wrap her arms around my waist. "You're another reason I love Dad. He gave me the best brother in the world."

My eyes didn't sting with unshed tears.

Well, maybe just a little.

Reese

Blaire got us each a Mai Tai from under the cabana and led me over to a couple of lounge chairs. She pointed at the rock waterfall. "You don't want to miss this."

I turned my attention to the waterfall as I took a sip of my drink. Nate Finlay was on top of the rock again, but this time, he was holding the hand of an older man. Even without the slender, muscular body covered in tattoos and the gold bracelets on his arms, I knew that man.

"Dean Finlay," I said. I had known he would be here, but seeing him like this was not something I expected.

"Yep," Blaire replied in an amused tone.

Nate yelled "Go!" and both of them dove into the water.

"He's been trying to get Dean to flip with him, but Dean won't do it. Said he'd break something important if he tried."

I laughed, thinking of how funny it would be to see Dean flipping off a rock waterfall.

"You took my chair," a deep male voice said behind me. I recognized it instantly.

I wasn't sure if I should look up and meet his gaze or what. I still couldn't figure out why he was even here. I kept waiting for Mase to notice him and say something, but he never did.

"Be nice, Captain. If you want to join us, you can have that seat." She pointed to one on the other side of me.

Captain? But I thought his name was River Kipling. Neither of those names sounded like Captain.

"Reese, this is my brother, Captain. He's a smart-ass one hundred percent of the time," Blaire said.

Her brother? What?

"Not a smart-ass, Sis. Told you I just say what I'm thinking. I don't beat around the bush. No point in wasting breath."

Blaire let out a chuckle and rolled her eyes. "He's actually a nice guy once you get to know him."

I had met him before, and I disagreed about him being a nice guy. But the guy I met had lied about his name.

"I, uh . . ." Should I tell Blaire I had met him before?

"What she's trying to say is she's met me already. We were at the same party my newest business partner was throwing. However, I introduced myself as River Kipling." He turned to me. "That's my given name. Captain is a nickname."

Blaire's eyes widened as she sat up straighter. "Really?"

I nodded. I wanted to add that he was an ass then, too, but I didn't. I liked Blaire. I didn't want to insult her brother.

"Your boyfriend been dancing any more with his cousin?" Captain, River, whatever his name was, asked.

I really didn't like this guy. I managed a tight smile and shook my head no. Although they *had* gone horseback riding and to a cattle auction together. I had told Mase to do both in hopes that I could win Aida over as the laid-back girlfriend, but it didn't do any good. She still glared at me or shot me triumphant little grins whenever she left the house alone with Mase, like she had won some sort of competition. It was incredibly weird.

"I'd watch that," he said. "I asked Hawkins about them, and he said Aida wasn't really Mase's cousin. She's his stepfather's niece, and she's also adopted. Girl looks like she has her eyes on your man."

"Captain, that's enough. Mase is very taken with Reese. She's moved to Dallas to live with him. And the way he watches over her is the same way Rush watches over me. Don't go giving her things to worry about."

I appreciated Blaire's words, but if what Captain said was true, then . . . was it possible Aida felt more for Mase than just a family bond? Did she want more? I cringed at the thought. That would be so messed-up if it were true.

"You ain't seen his cousin," Captain said in response to Blaire's remarks. "Long blond hair, all legs and curves. She's something to look at."

What the heck? Was he trying to scare me? And why did this man dislike me so much? I hadn't done anything to him. From the moment I met him, he'd been rude.

"So, Reese, what do you do out there on a ranch all day?" Blaire asked, obviously trying to change the subject.

Other than have sex with Mase, walk around, and clean, I did nothing, really. I needed to do something. I didn't like living off Mase. I wanted to make my own money, and I wanted to get my GED. It was something I planned on talking to Mase about when we got back. I needed a plan for life.

"I visited my family in Chicago for a month, but ever since I got back, I've just been spending time with Mase and hanging around the ranch. I need to get a job first thing we're back. I haven't started looking yet, but I'm thinking maybe cleaning work. And I'd like to go back to school." I didn't mention that school meant classes to get my GED, followed by an online college program, if I could save enough.

"Do you enjoy cleaning houses?" Blaire asked.

Not really, but for so long, it was all I could do. Now that I could read better, I had other options. I was just worried about whether I could focus on reading and writing in a pinch if I got stressed out on the job. "It isn't my dream job, but I'm good at it. If something better came along, I'd take it. I want to move on from cleaning houses."

Blaire smiled. "Yeah, I wanted to move on from being a cart girl when I worked at the golf course, so I completely understand."

"Reese." Mase's voice was a relief, and I looked up to see him standing in front of me. His gaze shifted from me to Captain.

"Kipling, was it?" he said, looking confused and a little angry.

"Colt, was it? I hear it's actually Manning," Captain replied, and he looked up at Mase with a bored expression.

"Mase, this is my brother, Captain, but his real name is River Kipling," Blaire explained.

"Brother?" Mase asked, shooting her a curious glance.

She nodded. "Yep."

"Small world and all that shit," Captain said.

"Yeah," Mase agreed, then held out a hand to me. "Thank you, Blaire, for watching over my girl and giving her some company. Harlow's good and coming out to enjoy her daughter's party now."

Blaire looked relieved. "Good."

I slipped my hand into Mase's and stood up. "I enjoyed

talking with you," I said to Blaire, while avoiding eye contact with Captain.

I thought I heard a low chuckle at my obvious slight of him, but I ignored it.

"I'll be by the ranch next week with Hawkins to see the cattle operation," Captain said to Mase.

Mase nodded his head. "See you then."

I could tell I wasn't the only one who didn't like Captain River Kipling.

We walked across the yard, and Mase got me another drink. As he turned to hand it to me, his eyes focused on something, or someone, behind me.

"Kiro," he said simply.

Kiro. As in Kiro Manning. I'd watched Dean Finlay jump off a rock with his grandson into the water, and now Kiro Manning was standing behind me.

"Glad you made it. Harlow wanted you here," a deep voice replied.

Mase glared at him. "I've never let my sister down."

The man behind me made a *hmph* sound, and Mase's back went rigid. I reached over and ran a hand up his arm to try to calm him.

"You going to introduce me to your friend?" Kiro asked. I still hadn't turned to look back at him.

Mase gazed down at me, and I moved to face Kiro. He was just like all the photos I'd seen of him and moved the same way he did in the music videos. But he'd also abandoned his son for years. I couldn't forgive him for that.

"Kiro, this is my girlfriend, Reese. Reese, this is my father, Kiro Manning."

Kiro grinned at me and shook his head. "This boy doesn't introduce any girls as his girlfriend. You must be something else."

"Uh, it's, um . . . nice to meet you." Kiro smirked. It looked so much like Mase's smirk that I stared for a moment in fascination.

"I got to go find my granddaughter and see if I can't get her from Grant long enough to take her inside to see Emmy," he said, then walked off.

Mase didn't seem surprised by his father's abrupt departure at all. Instead, he touched my lower back and led me away. "Let's find something to eat."

Mase

Spending time with my sister and niece was nice, and I had missed them, but I was more than ready to get back to Texas with Reese. Having sex hadn't been easy in my sister's house, and I wanted Reese all to myself; Harlow kept taking her away from me. I knew Reese needed girlfriends—she had never really had any, and I wanted that for her—but I missed having her close.

Once we got back to our own house, I breathed a sigh of relief. I grabbed the bag out of Reese's hand and set it down before pulling her hard against me. I'd been tempted to do this on the plane, but I figured she'd be embarrassed that the attendant could hear us in the back, so I'd let her curl up on me and go to sleep.

But we were in the privacy of our home now, and I wanted her naked.

"Strip," I said, and I jerked my shirt over my head.

Reese laughed as she stood there and watched me unbuckle my jeans.

"Not kidding, baby. I need in you now."

She didn't laugh this time. Instead, she pulled off the

shirt she was wearing and slipped out of her skirt. Just what I needed.

"I'm not letting you out of that bedroom until tomorrow at the earliest," I warned.

She bit her bottom lip and finished slipping out of her panties. That sight never got old. "Prove it," she taunted me.

I picked her up and threw her over my shoulder. I slapped her bare ass, making her squeal. Once we were in the bedroom, I put her in the middle of the bed. "We fuck first, then I'll play," I promised her.

Reese flashed me a teasing grin and rolled over, sticking her bottom in the air as she got onto her hands and knees. I ran both hands over her plump bottom and down the backs of her thighs. "You wanted to fuck. So fuck me," she said, glancing back at me.

She was being brave. Making the first move. My sweet girl was being naughty. I fucking loved it. I bent over her and kissed her shoulder. "How do you want to be fucked, baby? Easy?"

Reese shook her head. "No. I want you to fuck me the way you want to."

That was a loaded answer. But the first thing I did was kiss my freckle. Reese giggled as I paid that spot extra attention before moving a hand up between the silkiness of her inner thighs.

"OK to fuck first? You sure?" I asked her as I ran my lips up where my hands had just been.

"Yes, Mase. Fuck first," she said, with a soft moan.

Her wish was my command.

I came up behind her, grabbing her hips and easing in, slowly at first, until she had taken all of me. Then I took what she wanted me to, but it wasn't until I heard her scream my name over and over as her body trembled that I let out my own shout of pleasure.

Arthur Stout was meeting me at the barn today. He had called yesterday, saying he wanted to talk to me about purchasing one of my older, well-broken quarters for his wife to use for the riding school she ran on their ranch. Normally, I only dealt with cattle when it came to the Stouts, but every once in a while, his wife needed a dependable horse for her classes. Arthur always came to me, and I had two for him to look at that I thought would fit Mrs. Stout's needs.

I had kissed Reese good-bye and left her in bed before the sun came up. It bothered me to know she would be there most of the day unless she came down to see me. She didn't need that seclusion. Aida had gone to visit Grandma Colt for a few days with my mother, and it had been a relief to know I wouldn't have to deal with her drama while I figured out how to make life fuller for Reese.

Arthur's F-450 pulled up, and I dusted the dirt off my hands and walked out to meet him. I'd bathed and brushed Buttercup and Rose for him to inspect. Both of them would be fourteen years old this year. They were the perfect age for new learners.

"Morning, Mase," Arthur called out as he walked down the hill to meet me.

"Morning," I replied, tilting my hat back so I could see him better.

"It's 'bout afternoon for a rancher, though, isn't it, boy?" He chuckled.

It was only nine in the morning, but he was right. We got up early enough for nine to be more like twelve for most folks. When he got to the hill, he looked out over my training ring and nodded. "Looks good. Things must be going well for you. Glad to see that."

"Yes, sir. Business is growing."

"Good, good," he said, then took off his hat and wiped the sweat from his forehead with his sleeve. "I'm here to see those horses like I called about, but I got another proposition for you, too. My wife's business is growing, and she's needing more help in the office part of things. Taking phone calls and making phone calls. Reading e-mails and answering them. Even just cleaning the tack and whatnot." He paused and put his hat back on his head. "I heard your girlfriend was looking for a job. I liked the girl, and I think she'd work well with Piper."

Where had he heard Reese was looking for a job? She hadn't said anything about it. I wasn't sure I wanted her on the Stouts' property, either. Not with Hawkins around.

"I'm not real sure she's looking for a job. She's not mentioned it. Don't know where you got that information, but she's going to look into going back to school. I appreciate the offer, though."

Arthur looked disappointed, but he nodded. "Understood. Just thought I'd check. Piper has interviewed a few women, and they've been . . . older and treated her like, er, well, let's just say it didn't work out. She needs someone more her age."

I nodded that I understood, but I wasn't entertaining this idea. "You ready to see the girls?" I said, and I headed toward the stalls without waiting for him to follow.

Reese wasn't looking for a job. If she was, she'd have told me. Wouldn't she?

Reese

I fluffed the pillows on the sofa one more time before I continued pacing the living room. All day, I'd cleaned and thought about how I was going to tell Mase that I wanted a job. I also wanted to get my GED and take online college courses, but in order to do all that, I needed a steady income.

Staying here all day was not going to be enough. Even with Mase's two-hour lunch break, I needed something to do with the rest of my day. Telling Mase I wanted to have my own money and pay my own way wasn't going to go well. I could just feel it. He would go all caveman and insist he could take care of me. I needed to go another route. I needed to emphasize that I wanted a purpose. I wanted to get out into the world and do something.

He was a reasonable man. He would see what I was saying and understand.

Before I could get more nervous, the door opened, and in walked Mase, looking dirty, sweaty, and very sexy. He was my own personal cowboy, and I loved that. Seeing the smile on his face was all I needed, wasn't it? That smile made everything else seem less important. Did I want to upset him? Did I want to argue tonight? Or just curl up in his arms and talk about other things? Things that made him happy.

Yes . . . no . . . ugh! I had to talk to him. I had to face this. It was my life. Our life. I had to find my direction in it.

"I want to get a job," I blurted out, for fear that I wouldn't say it if I waited. "I want to get a job and a GED and take college courses online."

There. I had said it.

Mase stopped and studied me. He didn't say anything for a moment, and I worried that I'd sounded ungrateful or unhappy. I wasn't unhappy. I loved him. I loved being with him. I just needed more than being here all the time.

"You want a job?" he asked. "Who have you mentioned that to?"

I shook my head. "Just you," I replied. I didn't think I'd said it to anyone else, but maybe I had told Blaire, or was it Harlow? I couldn't remember.

"Why do you want a job?"

"I want to make money. I don't want you paying for my school and"—I held my hands out—"everything. I want to contribute. Staying here all day is . . . it's not doing anything, really. I need to work. I need to get my GED."

Mase let out a sigh and put his hands on his hips as he studied his boots a moment. He was upset. I had upset him. This was what I didn't want to do. I had opened my mouth to apologize when he looked back up at me. "OK. I understand. How do you feel about answering phone calls and e-mails and cleaning horse stalls?"

What? Was he trying to give me a job? That wasn't what I meant. He didn't need me. He was making up a job for me. I had to feel more independent than this. I needed that security. "No, Mase. You can't make up a job for me. You don't need help. I have to get a job out in the world and bring money home."

A small grin tugged on his lips. "It wouldn't be for me."

"Huh?"

He reached down and pulled off his muddy boots and set them near the door, then walked toward me. "Arthur Stout's wife, Piper, gives horse-riding lessons at their stables. She needs an assistant. Arthur offered you the job today."

He reached for my hand and held it in his like he was examining a priceless treasure in his palm. "You'd have to answer phones and take notes. Write them down. You'd have to read e-mails and reply to them. I didn't tell Arthur about your dyslexia. That's something for you to tell Piper if you want this job. I believe you can do it. I believe you can be the best damn assistant in the world. But I need to know if *you* believe it."

A job that didn't involve cleaning toilets. An assistant job. In an office. Wow. That was more than I thought I could do. "I'd tell her," I assured him. "Yes, I want it. That would be a great job to have on my résumé."

He nodded. "I agree. And I think you can do it. I hate to think of you gone all day, but I also want you to be happy. I want you to have everything you want in life."

I wanted him. He was the most important thing. But I did want other things, too. This was the first step toward being my own person. Reaching up, I wrapped my arms around his neck and held him close. "Thank you. Thank you so much for this."

Mase kissed my head. "Don't thank me for wanting to make

you happy. I intend to keep you here. Whatever I need to do to make sure that happens, I'll do."

Smiling, I laid my head on his chest.

"I'm filthy," he said, running a hand down my hair.

"I don't care. I like you this way. You're my sexy cowboy."

Mase chuckled. "Sexy cowboy, huh?" I nodded, and he held me tightly against him. "Why don't I fix us some sandwiches, and then you can take a shower with me to make sure this cowboy gets all clean."

I pulled back and smiled up at him. "What kind of girlfriend would I be if I stayed here all day and didn't fix you any dinner?"

"I didn't smell anything," he said, looking toward the kitchen.

"Because the fish is battered, and the hushpuppies are all rolled up and ready to go. I was just waiting for you to fry them so they'd be nice and hot. Fix yourself some sweet tea. It won't take me but ten minutes to fry everything up. The coleslaw is already chilled in the fridge."

His eyes lit up. "Seriously? Fried fish? Hot damn. I'll wash up and set the table."

Grinning, I ran a finger down his dirty shirt. "Why don't you take a shower so you can be clean for dinner?"

"A shower with you sounds like more fun," he said, with a pouty look that made me want to follow after him.

"You'll enjoy eating if you're clean. We can always get dirty again later."

"Keep talking like that, and we won't be eating *until* later."

Giggling, I ran to the kitchen to grab the fish out of the fridge before he could grab me.

"Fine. But we're getting dirty later. You promised."

I flashed him a grin, then went about getting the oil hot.

Mase had left me early this morning, like always, but he came back around eight thirty to wake me up. Piper had been thrilled to hear that I wanted to come in and speak with her about the job. She was expecting me around eleven. Luckily, Piper didn't live by ranch hours. She liked her sleep.

He kissed me and reassured me that I could do this. He also said he would come get me at around ten forty to give me a ride there. I didn't have a car here, but I wasn't sure of my way around anyway. This was another thing I hadn't considered. How was I going to get to my job every day? I couldn't just walk.

Mase

I hadn't been able to just drop Reese off. I needed to be with her when she met Piper. I also wanted to hold her fucking hand through the whole interview, but I couldn't. If Reese needed to show Piper she could do this, then having me around, coddling her, wasn't going to help.

Piper had given Reese a genuine smile when we approached and had been very friendly. She must have seen my reluctance to leave, because she'd turned to me and told me that Reese was in good hands and she would give me a call later. That had been her hint for me to leave.

Reluctantly, I went back to the ranch. My mother's truck was in the driveway, which meant Aida was back. But Major's was parked right next to it. I hadn't seen him in at least two months. I headed up to the house, in need of some sweet tea and something to get my mind and my worries off Reese.

Opening the screen door, I stepped off the porch and into the small entrance that led directly to the kitchen. Major was sitting at the table with a plate full of biscuits and gravy. Aida was across from him, scowling about something. I glanced over at my mother, who was still working at the stove on what smelled like bacon.

"Little late in the day for breakfast, isn't it?" I asked, taking off my hat before my momma could fuss at me and hanging it on the rack by the door.

All three sets of eyes turned to me.

"Her favorite boy is home. She's gotta feed me," Major replied with a stupid grin. Sometimes I think he honestly believed that.

"Oh, stop it. But yes, Major's here, and he looked starved. I knew what would put some meat back on his bones," Momma said.

Major looked just like he did the last time I saw him. He was by no means starved.

"Sure he does," I drawled, rolling my eyes. "Can your second-favorite boy get some of that, too?" I asked.

I walked over and kissed Momma on the cheek, and she squeezed me around the shoulders the best she could. "You're my number one always, and you know it. Sit down, and let me feed you, too. I also want to know all about Reese's new job."

"Reese got a job?" Aida asked, her eyes wide with something I didn't recognize.

"You already put her to work? Damn, man, what's your deal? Woman like that belongs in a bed all day. Happy and taken care of," Major said, and I knew he meant it.

"Major Colt, that is enough. No talk like that at my table," Momma said sternly.

He winked and puckered his lips like he was directing a kiss at Momma, before taking another bite. As always, my mother laughed at his antics. If that had been me, she'd have backhanded me.

"Reese wanted a job. I didn't make her get one. And Piper Stout offered her one that I think she'll enjoy."

Major frowned and took a drink of his tea. "She gonna be working at the Stouts'?"

I nodded.

"You're stupid as sh—uh, I mean . . ." He stopped from cursing as his eyes lifted to my mother, who was glaring at him in warning.

"I think she and Piper will get along fine."

Major cocked an eyebrow. "Wasn't Piper I was referring to. You do remember Hawkins, right?"

That was my biggest concern, but I trusted Reese. There was no question there. I just didn't want Hawkins ever making her feel uncomfortable.

"If at any time he steps over the line, I will handle it. But I can't keep her locked up away from the world. She needs a life."

Major shrugged, then went back to eating. "Whatever. But dude, your woman is smoking."

Aida let out a short laugh, like she thought that comment was amusing. Both Major and I turned to her.

"What? You don't agree?" Major asked her. He was always up for a fight with Aida. While I was the cousin she grew up adoring, he was the cousin she grew up fighting with.

"She's fat. Have you seen her butt? No offense, Mase. It's just you could do better," Aida said, looking at me with what she thought was an apologetic smile. It wasn't.

"Aida! Reese is not fat. I can't believe you'd say something so harsh." Momma turned her disapproving gaze Aida's way.

Aida shrugged. "I'm sorry, I don't mean to be rude, but she is . . . she's a little too curvy."

Major let out a loud laugh. "I am so glad I came back here. I was missing this, and no one told me." He continued to cackle with laughter.

"Reese's backside happens to be the very thing that caught my interest. It's perfect, and it's mine. I never want to hear you say anything negative about her body or her again. Do you understand me?"

Aida's eyes went wide, and I realized I'd never talked to her so coldly or harshly before. But she'd said the wrong thing. Being cruel wasn't acceptable. Being cruel to Reese would completely turn me against her.

Major finally stopped laughing. "Reese has the body of a porn star, Aida. You have the body of a model. Women want your body. Men want Reese's. It's a simple fact. But seeing you get jealous and ugly about it is priceless."

Aida stiffened at his comment. "I'm not jealous!"

"Don't talk about my woman's body being like a porn star's, or we'll have to take this outside my momma's kitchen, and I'll shut you up myself," I warned Major.

"I'm not jealous of *her*!" Aida said forcefully.

"I was just making a comparison. It was the best I had," Major said with a shrug.

"Don't," I warned him again before he said something I couldn't forgive.

"Mase is my cousin! Why would I be jealous of who he dates?" Aida spat out angrily.

Major turned his attention back to Aida. "Because you've always been jealous of anyone who has taken his attention off you, be it me, Harlow, or, hell, a damn horse. Because ever since you turned sixteen and the hormones kicked in and you realized there's not one drop of blood shared between you two, you've been obsessed with him. He can't see it, because he doesn't see you that way. But I can see it. You do anything you can to get his attention. Problem is, you're missing the big picture. He sees you as his cousin and nothing more."

What? Where had Major come up with this? Aida didn't think of me like that.

Aida stood up and ran out of the kitchen without a word. *What the hell?*

"Someone needed to say it," Major said, then leaned back and took a drink of his sweet tea.

"I'd better go check on her," Momma said, turning off the stove. "You two can help yourself to the bacon."

I watched as Momma went out the door to look for Aida.

"You didn't know, did you?" Major asked.

Know what? That Aida had a thing for me? Fuck, no. "I don't think you're right," I told him.

He chuckled. "Yeah, I'm right. Did your momma correct me or reprimand me? No. She went after Aida. She knows I'm right, too. We all saw it. Just not you."

Shit. What was I supposed to do with this? I knew Aida had been different since I'd brought Reese home. When Aida wasn't around, I didn't think about her or worry over her like I did with Harlow. We weren't that close.

"She always wanted to do things with just you. 'Take me dancing, Mase.' 'Let's go riding, Mase.' 'Some boy broke my heart, hold me, Mase.' All that shit was ridiculous, but you did it anyway, never once realizing what she was after."

I didn't say anything, because . . . I was afraid he was right.

"Hell, it's a good thing it was you she wanted. If it had

been me, I'd have fucked her. I have no morals. Besides, she's adopted, so I'm not really related to her, either. And her legs are pretty damn nice."

Shaking my head, I stood up. I couldn't sit here and listen to this. I needed to be alone. Figure out how to talk to her now. She'd just made this awkward, and she needed to go home. I couldn't have her here around Reese anymore. Not with this crazy shit going on in her head.

Reese

"That man of yours is a fine specimen. Seeing him all cave-man and protective over you is hot," Piper said with a wink. She was dressed in skintight jeans, brown leather riding boots, and a flannel shirt that was tied at her waist, showing off her flat stomach. "This is the office you'd be working in," she said, pointing toward a large barn door. "Let's go on inside and talk."

"OK," I said, as she turned and headed for the door. I was nervous. Since the moment Mase had let go of my hand and left, my heart had been pounding in my chest and my throat felt tight. This was it. My chance at a job that could help me in life and really get me somewhere.

The door opened, and I took a moment to look around. The ceiling went all the way to the roof of exposed wooden beams. Large Edison bulbs hung from long cords from the ceiling, casting the room in flattering light. Bookshelves lined the back wall, and three tall file cabinets were against the left side of the room. A computer with a massive screen sat on a whitewashed wooden table. Two brown leather chairs were across from the desk, with a small round barrel functioning as an accent table between them.

Piper took a seat in one of the chairs and waved for me to take the other.

"So," she said, crossing her legs and draping an arm across her thigh. "Mase informed Arthur that you don't have any experience with horses or the type of work I would require. He did say that you were a hard worker and he believed you could do anything you put your mind to. What I want to know about is you. What you think you can do. What you want to do."

This was it. I would have to tell her about my dyslexia now. No point in going any further if this was unacceptable for her. I unclenched the tight fist in my lap and took a deep breath. I had nothing to be ashamed of. I was not stupid. I had learned to read, and my writing skills had improved ever since Mase began teaching me.

"First, I want you to know that I do have dyslexia." I didn't pause and give her time to say anything. "Until I met Mase, I couldn't read or write. He came into my life and helped me identify the root of my problem, and then he got me help. I read daily to him, and I also write daily in a journal, which Mase reads over to check my spelling. I've worked hard to get to where I am. However, when I'm in a tense situation and feel pressured, I can misspell something or possibly freeze up and not be able to write at all. I understand if this is something you don't think will work with your needs. However, I do want this job, and I will do my very best to make you happy."

Piper sat there a moment before speaking.

I focused on not fidgeting with my hands. I was nervous, but this was a part of my life. One I had to learn to work with.

"This job will require a lot of reading and writing. However, from what I've just heard, I think that having an employee who wants to do a good job and doesn't take it for granted is the best kind to have. I will need you to answer phone calls, take notes, read and reply to e-mails, and then help me some with the tack and cleaning the stalls. If you are up for this challenge, I want to offer it to you. I like fighters, Reese Ellis, and you seem like a fighter to me."

I could feel the tears sting my eyes, but I blinked them back. Relief washed through me, and I smiled. It was probably one of those big, cheesy grins, but I didn't care. I had gotten the job. Me. I had done this.

"Thank you," I said, wishing I had words to tell her how truly thankful I was.

Piper leaned over and patted my knee. "Don't thank me yet. You may hate this job, but I'm hoping you won't."

I wouldn't. I was going to love it. Because it was something I'd gotten on my own.

Sitting behind the desk, alone in the office, I checked the third thing off the list in front of me. Piper had gone over everything with me and then left me a list of things she needed me to do today. Once she had left, I'd let out a huge sigh of relief. Being in here alone made it so much easier to read and write. I had complete focus.

The next thing on the list was to read and reply to the e-mails. Piper got a lot of interest in her horseback-riding lessons. I'd already had four phone calls about it. When I opened the in-box, there were eight e-mail inquiries.

I began reading the first one but had barely made it through before the door opened after one short knock. I glanced up to see a familiar face but not one I had expected to see or wanted to see, for that matter. His messy, sun-streaked hair was pulled back again and covered by a backward baseball cap.

"You got the job," he said, with a smug look on his face.

How did he know about the job? I nodded but didn't say anything.

Captain chuckled and stepped into the office. "You like it?" he asked, looking as if he had every right to be standing in this room.

I nodded again.

His grin grew, and a dimple appeared on his face. "Is your silence a challenge, Reese? Because I like challenges."

Dang this man. He was determined to drive me crazy. "Actually, it was a hint for you to leave."

Captain gave me a smirk, stepped over to one of the leather chairs, and sank down into it. He stretched his long jeans-clad legs out in front of him, then crossed them at the ankle. "I was told to wait here for Piper. She's with a client. I need her signature on some forms, and Arthur is in Austin today. Piper has to sign when he's gone."

Great. I didn't know that seeing Captain . . . River . . . whatever I was supposed to call him was part of my job description.

I turned my attention back to the computer screen, but I could feel his eyes on me. I had a hard time concentrating. It felt like he was trying to memorize my every feature.

"Your man still running around with that cousin of his?"

I stiffened. Why was he so intent on making me think something that wasn't true about them? I knew that Mase loved me. I also knew that he didn't have a thing for Aida.

Although she might very well have a thing for him. "No, but that's not your business."

"Don't reckon it is. But I don't want to be too far away when he screws up. He's got something I want."

All the words on the screen blurred, and my head pounded. What was he talking about? Mase had something he wanted? Me? Was he talking about me? No. He liked to say things to upset me. He didn't flirt with me. He was an asshole. "You'll be waiting a long time. Mase doesn't mess up. He's the best man I know," I said, staring at the jumbled words on the screen. My focus was completely gone.

"No man's perfect, sweetheart," he drawled.

I didn't like him calling me sweetheart. I also hated him insinuating that Mase could do something wrong. Something to hurt me. He wasn't like that. Just because Captain River Whoever was a jerk, that didn't mean all men were jerks.

"Mase is," I replied tightly.

He didn't respond right away, and I tried to take a deep breath and focus on the words. Pretend he wasn't there. "He saved you? Is that why you trust him so much? You needed a savior, and he came along at the right time. Is that it?"

Yes, he saved me. He loved me. But that wasn't this man's business. Nothing in my life was this man's business. "He changed my world."

Captain let out a sigh that caught my attention, and I turned to look at him. He stood up, and I hoped that meant he was leaving. I had work to do. He was messing with that. "I can change your world, too, sweetheart. But I'll wait my turn," he said, then walked out the door without another word.

I stared at the closed door with mixed feelings of disbelief, confusion, and anger. Who did he think he was? And why was he interested in me? It wasn't like he couldn't walk into a room and crook his finger at any girl he wanted. He needed to find someone who was actually available.

Mase

The smile that lit Reese's face when I opened her office door made all the pain of missing her and worrying about her fade away. To see her smile like that, sitting behind such a nice desk, made it all worth it. She was happy.

"I did it. I did everything on my list," she said, with pride in her voice.

I walked over to her as she stood up and reached for her purse.

Pulling her into my arms, I held her close and inhaled her scent before covering her mouth with mine. I needed a taste before we went back to my truck for the ride home. Her hands came up and clung to my arms. I loved it when she did that. Like she needed to hold on to me.

When I had enough to get me home, I pressed one last kiss to her lips and moved my head back so that I could take her in. "I'm so proud of you."

She beamed at me. "I'm proud of me, too."

That. That was all I needed. Anything she wanted to do, I'd make it happen if I could hear those words from her mouth. She had a lot to be proud of. I never wanted her to doubt herself again.

"Ready to go home?" I asked.

She slipped her purse over her shoulder. "Yes."

I put my hand on her lower back, and we walked out the door. She turned and locked it with her new set of keys, then glanced up at me. "Piper left early. She said she'd see me tomorrow, so I don't have to let her know I'm gone."

Good. The sooner I got her home, the better.

On the ride home, she talked about her day and all the e-mails and phone calls she'd gotten. She sounded excited, like she had enjoyed every minute of it. I let her happiness push away my own feelings about the day I'd had out of my mind. Aida had stayed gone all day. Momma said I just needed to give her some space to deal. She said it was time Aida got over this crush she had on me. Major bringing it up was the best thing that could have happened to her. She had to get over it now and move on.

That didn't make it easier, and I was concerned about where Aida had run off to. She was young and so naive and silly about things. The fact that she had a crush on me proved that even more. I didn't want her going out and getting hurt because of this. I'd blame myself.

When we pulled into the driveway, Aida's truck was sitting there. Looked like I was going to face this sooner rather than later, and I didn't want Reese hearing any of it. Aida was sitting in the driver's seat with her head on the steering wheel like she was crying. Great.

I parked the truck and looked over at Reese, who was staring at Aida. I never wanted Reese to know that Aida had a thing for me. That was something I had to shut down now so we could get on with things. Reese's emotions weren't going to be messed with here. I had to protect her first.

"I need to talk to her. She's going through something right now, and I'm the only one who can help her move on," I explained. I wanted to go inside and eat dinner with Reese, then enjoy a long shower together before we curled up and she read to me. But that wasn't happening tonight. I had to put this behind us.

She nodded. "OK. I'll go fix us some dinner."

The tone in her voice sounded off, but I was probably imagining things, since I was already worried about this shit with Aida. I leaned over and kissed her before getting out of the truck.

Reese climbed down before I could get to her. "Go do what you need to," she said, and she walked up the stairs without looking back at me.

That wasn't like Reese. Maybe she was just tired and ready to go inside. I wanted to go with her. Shit, this was all kinds of fucked-up.

I walked over to the driver's-side door of Aida's truck and opened it. "Move over, I'm driving," I said when she lifted her tear-streaked face to look at me.

She didn't question me. Once she was on the other side, I climbed in. "Put on your seat belt," I told her when she didn't reach for it.

Once she was buckled, I pulled out of the driveway and drove to the main road. We needed to talk, but I was going to drive while we did it. I needed something to do other than look at her and face this shit.

"Talk, Aida. Stop crying, and talk to me."

She sniffled, and I watched her wipe at her face. "What do you want me to say? Major said it all."

Well, that clarified that. "What the hell, Aida? Seriously? How did this happen?"

She let out a shaky sigh. "You were . . . *are* my everything, Mase. You always have been. You're there when I need someone. We have fun together. We laugh. We fit. I just don't know why you can't see that. She . . . she doesn't fit you. I do. I know you so much better than she does."

Motherfucker. How had I missed this? I felt so blindsided. "You're my cousin. Hell, Aida, I saw you a couple times a year growing up. It wasn't like we were inseparable. The way you talk about us sounds like we did everything together. I don't see how you cooked all this up in your head. I've never once given you reason to think we have something or even *had* something. We hardly see each other."

Aida sighed. "You don't see it. We've always had a connection. I could feel it. I know you did, too. Reese messed this all up. You think you love her. You just don't remember what we've had together."

Yes, I loved Reese. I loved Reese like a man insane. She was my world. That wasn't ever changing. "Aida, Reese is everything I never knew I needed but I can't live without. Telling yourself that there is, or was, something between us is pointless. You've always been jealous of others getting my attention. I knew that. But we were kids, and you were demanding. I overlooked it or ignored it. But this can't be ignored. Reese is the most important person in my life."

Aida let out another sob. "Why can't that be me? What

does she have that I don't have? How can I be her? How do I win your love?"

Holy hell. "You can't. It doesn't work that way. You can't be like her and win my love. Reese is my one. You will find a guy one day who will be that for you, and no one will ever compare."

"I don't want anyone else. I never have," she said in a sad voice.

"I'm trying to be understanding here, but you're making it hard. I don't get it. This isn't healthy, Aida. You've got to see that."

She began crying softly again, and I just drove. She had to see the truth here and deal with it. The lights of Fort Worth appeared in the distance. I hoped a coffee shop was open, because I needed something to get me through this.

"What if she isn't your forever? What if one day she leaves? Or you fall out of love with her? You don't know the future. No one does. People break up, and they even get divorced. What about when you don't love her anymore?"

None of that was happening, and hearing her even mention it pissed me off. "Not me. That isn't me. I don't give up. I'd never give up on her."

Aida laid her head back on the seat and let out a frustrated groan. "You're so stubborn."

I almost laughed. She was calling me stubborn. Seriously? "This has got to end, Aida. I'm not kidding. Reese is mine. She's my happiness. My reason for waking up in the morning. She is every smile on my face. That's it. Nothing will change that."

Aida closed her eyes as I pulled into a Starbucks drive-through. A beer would be better, but I had to drive, so a black coffee was going to have to suffice. "You want anything?" I asked her.

"No," she said sulkily.

I ordered mine, and we sat there in silence. Once I had my drink I turned back toward the ranch.

"She'll leave you one day, and I'll be gone. You'll regret this. I swear you will," Aida said, looking out the window.

The only thing I would regret was that I had missed all the signs and let it get this far gone. Aida needed to go home. Her visit was over. I hoped it would be years before her next one.

When I finally got home after dropping Aida back at my parents' house, I'd been gone for more than two hours. Aida had wanted to talk more, and I had listened, but I didn't feel like I had made any progress with her. She was still warning me that I was messing up. I was beginning to think my cousin was mentally unbalanced.

As I opened the door, the smell of garlic and butter met my nose. Walking into the kitchen, I could see spaghetti simmering in a pot of boiling water on the stove. Toasted French bread rubbed with garlic and butter sat beside it.

But Reese wasn't there.

I headed for the bedroom, and just as I reached the door, I heard her voice. I stopped and realized she was reading. Alone. Without me.

She had worked her first day at a new job, and I'd left her here. Instead of pouting like most women would, she had cooked dinner and was now going on with her night. My gut knotted up. I felt like an ass. I should have been here with her. I should have cooked for her. And I should be there holding her while she read. That was our thing.

Opening the door, I stepped into the room, my eyes instantly finding her. She was curled up in our bed, with her hair in low pigtails and dressed in a tank top and pajama pants. She stopped reading and looked up at me.

Then she smiled.

That smile was all that I needed in life. That and having her right there in my bed. Nothing was as perfect as this.

"I'm sorry," I said, needing to say it. My guilt and regret over leaving her was eating at me.

She shrugged. "It's OK. She needed you."

But so did Reese. I never wanted to choose someone else's needs over Reese's. "I should have been here with you. I should have cooked you dinner and listened to you talk about your day. And I should be in that bed listening to you read to me."

Reese put her book down in her lap. "I would have liked that."

Those honest words sliced through me. That ride with Aida did nothing but let me say how I felt. I'd wasted my time. And I'd let Reese down.

"I have to get up early. I'd like to stay up with you while you eat and shower, but Piper needs me at the office at eight tomorrow morning. She signed on for some earlier lessons, so I need some sleep."

Although she said everything with a smile, there was a sadness in her eyes that made me feel helpless. Then she lay down and rolled over, ending our conversation.

I had screwed up.

Reese

When my alarm went off at six thirty, I rolled over and stretched. Last night's events, and the sadness I'd gone to bed with, came back to me. Mase had gone to Aida and stayed gone for hours. I had waited to eat with him for more than an hour, until I was too hungry to wait. Once I'd eaten and cleaned up, I took a shower, and he still wasn't home.

By the time I'd gotten my book and started reading, I realized this was a pattern. When Aida needed him, he went to her. It concerned me. She wasn't his blood relative, but he had never told me that. Someone else had.

I shook my head, threw back the covers, and got out of bed. I had to focus on work today. Not Mase. Not Aida. That was a situation I needed to find my way through. I hoped going to sleep on him when he got home last night sent the right message. He had upset me. I wanted him to know that. I didn't want to take a backseat to his cousin forever.

He was my first concern. Shouldn't I be his?

I went to brush my teeth and get dressed. Today was about proving my worth at my job, not sulking because Mase had let me down last night.

When I stepped out of the bedroom, my eyes fell on Mase

standing at the stove. His back was to me, but he was definitely cooking. I walked toward the kitchen through the living room, hoping to see what he was doing.

Mase turned just as I got into the kitchen and gave me that smile that made my heart flutter. "Morning, beautiful. Breakfast is almost done."

Breakfast? We normally ate cereal or something his mom, Maryann, brought us. And wasn't Mase supposed to be down at the stables working?

"Have a seat, and I'll get your orange juice," he said, wiping his hands on the dishtowel stuck in the front of his jeans.

I didn't move. I was still trying to figure out what was going on.

He paused when he saw me still standing there. "You good?" he asked, looking concerned.

I managed a nod and moved to the table while he poured me a glass of orange juice.

"Coffee is brewing. I'll get you some in a few."

"What are you doing?" I blurted out.

He slid what looked like an omelet from a pan to a plate, then turned to me and held it up. "Fixing you breakfast. I didn't get to make you dinner after your first day of work. So I thought I'd fix you breakfast before your second day. Not the same, but I didn't sleep much last night. I watched you sleep and beat myself up over letting you down." He walked over to me with a serious expression on his face. When he set the plate down in front of me, he bent over and looked into my eyes. "I never want to be the one to let you down, and I did that last night. I won't do it again. You're the most important part of my life."

My heart went into a silly beat of giddiness. I had been upset with him, but this made all that melt away. This was Mase. The man I trusted and loved. I returned his smile. "Thank you," I whispered.

He leaned in and kissed me sweetly. "Don't thank me. I don't deserve it," he said against my mouth. "Be mad at me. Throw things at me. Hell, baby, slap me. But don't thank me. That kills me."

I reached up and cupped his face. I adored that face. "How about I love you, then?" I said with a smile.

He closed his eyes and leaned into my hand. "That always sounds good."

I moved my hand and looked down at the plate in front of me. The omelet he'd made looked delicious and full of cheese, but it was also big enough for three people. "Go get another plate and eat with me. This is massive."

He chuckled. "Yeah, I guess it is."

During our breakfast, I told him everything I had wanted to tell him last night. He told me about his day, although I felt like he was leaving something out. It was in his eyes. And he never told me what Aida had come over for.

That bothered me.

The morning had gone by quickly. Piper was busy with one lesson after another, and I had to go out and help her do some cleaning and brush down the horses. She'd explained how to do it and showed me once yesterday, and I had picked it up quickly. I was feeling very accomplished by the time lunchtime rolled around.

I hadn't packed a big lunch today, and I was starving. My turkey sandwich and apple would not be enough. I wanted a big, thick hamburger and a large order of fries. Not that my butt needed it, but I sure wanted it. Maybe even some chocolate chip cookies. I would have to use my imagination and eat the sandwich I'd brought and pretend it was something yummier.

"You have something to eat?" Piper asked, sticking her head through the doorway.

Not what I wanted. "Yes," I replied.

"Good. Take your lunch break. I'm headed up to the house to meet Arthur for lunch. See you later this afternoon."

I nodded, and she closed the door behind her. Sighing, I pulled out my paper bag and set it on my desk. Tomorrow I would prepare a huge lunch. Something delicious. Something wonderful.

The door opened again, and I looked up, expecting to see Piper again, but it wasn't my boss. It was someone else. Someone I did not want to see.

"Piper just left for lunch," I said, sounding more annoyed than necessary.

Captain grinned, and I noticed his dimple again. Were guys supposed to have dimples like that? It was a deep one.

"Brought lunch," he said, holding up a large paper bag. Much bigger than mine.

"I didn't ask for lunch," I snapped.

My attitude didn't deter him. He walked into the office and closed the door behind him. "No, you didn't, but I was getting mine, and I thought what the hell. Do something nice for someone today, Captain." He set the bag on my desk. The smell of something mouthwatering hit my nose. Much better than my sandwich. "So when I ordered the best damn burger in Texas, I decided to get two and bring one to you. Day two on the job, figured you needed a treat."

He had brought me a burger. Was he kidding me? Did this man read minds?

When he placed the large box in front of me, I was pretty sure I was drooling. It smelled amazing. He was just being nice. Who was I to turn down a lunch that I had just been dreaming about?

"I was expecting more snarky comments. Possibly a threat to throw the damn burger right in my face. That kind of thing," Captain said, sounding smug.

I should have done all those things, but I wanted the food. The idea of eating my turkey sandwich now was just sad.

"To sweeten the deal, I got you a slice of strawberry cake," he added. Not chocolate chip cookies, but that was a good substitute. He opened my box as if I couldn't do it.

"You win. I'm starving."

He laughed then. A real laugh. Not one that was all-knowing or assholish. I liked his laugh. It wasn't bad. Not nearly as annoying as he was in general.

"Well, thank you. This means my good deed for the day is complete and I can go about my business being a bastard."

This time, I laughed.

When he pulled up a chair and started opening up his food, I realized he was staying. I wasn't sure about that. It seemed a little too familiar. We weren't friends. We weren't anything.

"Just eat, Reese. I'm not going to come across the table and grab you. I'm just eating before my food gets cold."

Right. OK.

I watched as he picked up his burger and took a bite. It looked so good. I pushed my concerns aside and did the same.

We ate in silence, and I decided this was OK. Not weird at all. And the burger was the best thing I'd put in my mouth. The fries were also fulfilling my fantasies. When I had almost finished, he spoke again.

"You hang out at home alone last night? Since your man was off getting coffee with his cousin?"

He'd gone to get coffee with her? I had thought she was crying. They'd stayed out late having coffee? "She was upset. He was trying to comfort her," I said, pushing the food away. I wasn't hungry anymore. Not even the temptation of the strawberry cake appealed to me.

"Uhhh, she didn't seem upset when I saw them. I even saw him laugh. Shame he left you at home at night. It was your first day at work. He should have been there with you."

"Stop it," I said, standing up and putting distance between us. I didn't want to listen to him voice my own fears. It was enough for me to hear them in my head.

He closed his box and leaned back in his chair to look at me. "You don't deal well with the truth, do you?"

"I'm fine with the truth," I replied, my voice rising. He was getting to me. He was making me angry again. He was good at that.

"Then why does me telling you what I saw and how I think it was wrong upset you? I'm just speaking the truth. Any man who has you at home should keep his ass right there with you."

No, no, no. I was not listening to this. He was saying these things to make me doubt Mase. I would not doubt Mase. I'd done that once and almost ruined everything. "He felt bad for leaving me. He apologized over and over and even made me breakfast this morning. Mase is a good man. He loves me. Stop trying to make me doubt him."

Captain stood up and kept his heated gaze on me. He wasn't smirking now or looking like he was about to say something else snarky. It was the first real expression I'd seen on him. "I'm not trying to upset you. I'm trying to show you that not all men are what they seem to be. No one is, sweetheart. I've seen it too many times. And the first time I looked into your eyes, I saw a pain I understood. Before you opened your mouth and enchanted my hard, bitter soul, I wanted to protect you. I can't help that."

I didn't have words. He had to go. This was not an innocent lunch. "Leave, please," I said, pointing at the door.

He didn't argue. He simply nodded his head, turned, and walked out.

I stood there staring at that closed door for several minutes. He was dangerous. I couldn't let him get near me again. I didn't want his honesty. I didn't want his truths. I just wanted Mase.

Mase

Something was bothering Reese. From the time I'd picked her up this afternoon, she had seemed off. Her smile didn't meet her eyes. She also seemed clingy. Not that I was complaining. But she didn't let me get far from her. We had showered together and had sex on the bathroom counter before moving to the sofa and curling up together.

She was currently sitting in my lap with her arm around my shoulders and her head on my chest. The guilt about last night was still digging at me. Was that why she was acting so differently? She was worried I'd leave her again? Did she think she had to hold on to me? I fucking loved it when she clung to me, but I didn't want her doing it because she felt like she had to.

I wanted her to know I was always hers. No need to cling to me. I wasn't going anywhere. I trailed my fingertips over her bare thighs, thinking about all we'd been through and how far she'd come.

She had grown so much, and I would never forgive myself if my stupid actions took that away from her. She was mine, but I was just as much hers. No one else would have me this way.

"I love you," I whispered into her hair.

"I love you, too," she replied, and traced a heart on my chest with her finger.

"I won't leave you again," I told her. I needed her to believe me.

She didn't reply. Instead, she continued tracing that heart on my chest over and over.

"You own me, Reese. Know that, baby. Know that I'm yours."

She stopped tracing on my chest and tilted her face up to look at me. "What if, one day, you're not mine anymore and you can't help it?"

What did she mean by that? "I can swear to you that you will always be it for me. No one fits me like you. No one makes me feel whole. No one else ever will."

She smiled and pressed a kiss to my chest. "I want to believe that."

Well, fuck me. I wanted her to believe that, too. I thought she did. Had my one stupid mess-up last night made her doubt that? Doubt me?

I cupped her face and held her so that she was looking directly into my eyes. "Do you see me? This man in front of you will love you until the day he dies. You're my one, Reese. My one."

She relaxed in my arms and leaned into me. "OK."

OK? Ha! That was all she was going to say? OK?

"Does that 'OK' mean you believe me?"

She nodded. "I believe you. I always believe you."

Pulling her tight against my chest, I held on to her. This was my home. She was where my home would always be. It was time I took the next step and proved to her that I was all in. Forever.

Reese was talking to her father on the phone this morning. She didn't have to go to work until nine, so she had called her dad to catch him up on things. Checking in with family wasn't something Reese was used to doing. I expected him to want her to come visit again soon, and I needed to prepare the ranch for my absence. She wasn't going without me again.

"Yes, I love it there. Piper, my boss, is really great. And I learned to brush down the horses," she said, chatting away happily.

Just hearing her made me smile. I hadn't been sure how I felt about him walking into her life like he had at first. I'd been afraid he was out for something. But he hadn't been. He'd honestly wanted to know his daughter. Reese had needed that more than I even realized. The horror from her past seemed to be fading away for her, though I knew it would always be a part of her in some way. She just wasn't letting it define her life. She didn't use her mother and her stepfather as excuses not to achieve more. Reese believed in herself.

After I dropped Reese off at work, I went to Momma's. I hadn't talked to her since the Aida thing. I knew Aida's truck was gone, but I didn't ask about it. Seeing her gone was more of a relief.

Major's truck was still there, though. He'd been gone all day yesterday, but apparently, he hadn't left town. I parked my truck and headed inside.

Major was drinking a cup of coffee and eating again. "What

do you think this is? A bed-and-breakfast?" I grumbled, walking inside to go kiss my momma and get myself a cup of coffee.

"Don't be hating. There's plenty for you, too," he said with a mouth full of food.

"Good morning, son," Momma said.

"Morning, Momma."

"Reese at work?" she asked.

I nodded and took a sip of the hot liquid.

"Did you tell her your cousin has the hots for you?" Major asked.

If we hadn't been in Momma's kitchen, I'd have put my fist in his face.

"Major," Momma warned.

He held up both hands. "Just asking."

"Aida went back to her parents' house. She took off from college this semester, and they're going to force her to make it up this summer. Her daddy is not happy that she took off to come here," Momma explained. "But she's young, and she'll learn. Let's just put this behind us."

"So you didn't tell Reese, did you?" Major asked, grinning.

I glared at him over my coffee cup.

"I wouldn't have told her, either. It's creepy, if you really think about it."

"Would you shut up?" I growled.

He stood up with his empty plate and headed to the sink. "Sure. I'll shut up. I got a job to get to."

"Job?" I asked, surprised.

"Yep. I'm working on building the addition to Stouts and Hawkins. His new guy overseeing the project, River Kipling, hired me. If this one is as successful as the one in Key West, then Arthur is sending him to Rosemary Beach to build another, and I'll be going, too. Find me one of those hotties I've heard so much about."

The idea of River Kipling moving to Florida, far away from Dallas, was very appealing.

Reese

Piper walked into the office an hour after I had arrived, carrying two cups of coffee. "Good morning," she said brightly.

As weird as it was to imagine her married to Arthur, a man who could be her father, I really liked Piper. She was down-to-earth, and I'd watched her with the kids she trained. She was kind. I felt guilty now for thinking Arthur had married her for her beauty and youth while she'd married him for his money. I didn't get that vibe from Piper.

"Good morning," I replied, taking the coffee cup she handed to me. "Thank you. I need this."

"Everyone always needs a good cup of coffee." She took one of the leather seats across from the desk. "So, tell me, how are you liking this job?"

I loved working here. I felt I was being productive. "I'm enjoying it very much."

Piper sipped from her cup and smiled at me over the rim. "Good," she said. "I'm very happy with your work. Everything you've done you've given one hundred percent. You work like you own it and it means something to you. That's hard to find in an employee. I hope I can keep you around for a while."

"Thank you," I replied, feeling my chest swell with pride. I had been so worried I wouldn't be able to do this job correctly, but here she was telling me she was impressed with my work. I could do this. Mase was right. He believed in me, and I needed to start believing in me, too.

"Now that you've shown me you can handle the daily tasks, I need to add one more thing to your list. My husband has a guy working on building and expanding the menu to include seafood at his steakhouse here in Dallas, which he has already done successfully in Key West. River Kipling. He's asked for some help filing his receipts and bills. Until the expansion is complete, Arthur needs to use my extra filing cabinet to organize all of that. We'll need you to file the paperwork that River brings in, and he'll occasionally ask you to make phone calls on his behalf while he's on-site."

Oh, no. How could I tell her I didn't want to work with River? She'd just said I was doing a great job and wanted me around for a while. I couldn't refuse to do this. Besides, he would just be dropping stuff off every once in a while. Not a big deal. I was making more out of this than I needed to.

"OK, sure," I replied, not feeling sure at all.

She gave me an approving smile and took one last drink of her coffee before standing up. "He should be by sometime before lunch to go over things with you. I told him you'd be expecting him."

Today? Already? I needed more time. I nodded. It was all I could do.

"Great. Well, back to work. I have a student arriving in about five. Enjoy your morning, Reese."

I think I muttered something about her enjoying her morning, too, but I wasn't sure. My mind was on dealing with

River . . . or Captain. I needed to tell Mase about this. He needed to know that I'd be seeing River more often—but then what? He would be furious, and I'd probably lose this job.

I liked my job. I wouldn't get a better one. Having this on my résumé was going to introduce me to more opportunities.

At some point, I was able to get my mind off of Captain long enough to focus on my calls and e-mails. I brushed down two horses for Piper and made another pot of coffee and brought her a cup. Just before I was ready to take my lunch and after Piper had left to eat with her husband, my office door opened. I knew without looking up who it would be.

Same messy hair in a ponytail, same smart-ass grin. I only gave him a glance before I looked back down at my computer screen and finished reading an e-mail. Or at least tried to.

"Are you mad about this arrangement?" he asked, walking over to set a bag on my desk.

I couldn't ignore him; Piper had asked me to help him out. I forced myself to look at him. "What do you have for me?" I asked, inwardly cringing.

He smirked. "First, I have some of the best Mexican food in Dallas for you. Once we eat, we can get to the other stuff."

He had brought me food again. This wasn't just friendly—I knew that. He was trying to flirt with me. But I was Mase's, and this wasn't going to work. "I've already eaten," I lied.

Captain shook his head as if he was disappointed in me. "I'm not a fan of liars."

Ugh. This man pissed me off. "Let's just get to business. What do you need me to file?" I wasn't going to play this cat-and-mouse game or whatever it was he was trying to do with me.

He opened the bag and pulled out the most delicious-smelling taco in the world. He unwrapped it before taking a bite and sitting down in one of the chairs across from me. What was he doing, trying to torture me? "It's my lunch break. Thought I'd share with you, but since you want to pretend like you've already eaten, I'm sure you won't mind if I eat in front of you. I'm starving."

Fantastic. I tried to breathe through my mouth so I couldn't smell the delicious taco, but I could already taste it. And I wanted some. Swinging my gaze back to my computer screen, I reread the same sentence three times, and each time it said something different. He was making me feel flustered, and I didn't like it.

"Could you toss me another taco?" he asked, and I jerked my gaze up to see him wadding up the empty wrapper.

"I wasn't aware my new role included feeding you. Get it yourself," I snapped.

This only made him laugh. I could see him out of the corner of my eye stand up and get another taco out of the bag. He stood there and unwrapped it, then placed it right in front of me before reaching in to get another and taking his seat across from me again. "Damn good tacos," he said.

I tried not to look down at the taco. Why was he so determined to feed me? And why did he always bring good things to eat? Why couldn't he bring something I didn't like? Things would be much easier that way.

"Just eat it, Reese. It's not a marriage proposal; it's a motherfucking taco, for crying out loud."

I shot him an angry glare, then gave in and picked up the taco to take a bite. I didn't look at him, and he didn't gloat in triumph. We sat there silently, and I finished off the taco, although I felt a tug of guilt with each bite.

"One more?" Captain asked.

I figured I'd already had one so I might as well have two. We didn't talk. We didn't argue. It was peaceful, and I was hoping the business side of our relationship would go just as smoothly.

He cleaned away our taco feast and then pulled out a large envelope and placed it in front of me. "This first batch is a mess, and there are a lot of receipts. I'll try to get them to you every couple of days so this doesn't happen again. Also, do you have a cell phone? I need to be able to text you when I have calls I need you to make for me."

I did have a cell phone, but I wasn't sure that having him text me was a good idea. I just stared up at him silently.

He sighed and raised his eyebrows while giving me that exasperated look. "Would you rather I text you or visit you every time I need you to make phone calls?"

I quickly gave him my number, which made him chuckle.

"I'll be here on Monday to go over some other things I need filed and categorized separately."

I nodded. Could he leave now?

Captain gave me a smirk, then turned to go. "Enjoyed lunch with you," he said, just before he walked out of the office. He always got the last word. It was annoying.

Mase

"Friday night. Come on, man. Reese will enjoy a good honky-tonk. You haven't been with me in ages. Let's drink up, play some pool, and dance. It'll be fun." Major badgered me as he sat on the fence post while I worked on one of my new quarter horses, Bingo.

I was more than positive that Reese would not enjoy a honky-tonk. I ignored Major's suggestion for the fifth time in a row. "Don't you have a job to do?" I asked, annoyed that he'd decided to come bug me.

"I go in after two. Hey, let's go bowling. I can whup both your asses."

I shot him a glare. I wasn't going fucking bowling. "Are you lonely? Is that what this is? You done with Cordelia already?"

He frowned like he wasn't sure what I was talking about. "Cordelia? Hell, man, I haven't seen her in a month or more. It wasn't like I wanted to put a ring on it. She was just a good fuck."

Rolling my eyes, I went back to work. He was impossible to talk to sometimes.

"You're gonna miss me when I'm in Florida. You know you will. Might as well get all the Major you can while I'm here."

"I get enough of you as it is. You're always in my momma's kitchen stuffing your face."

"Awww, are you jealous because she loves me more?"

"No . . . but are you sleeping with your dad's new girlfriend yet?" I retorted, thinking that would piss him off. He'd contributed to the end of his dad's last marriage by sleeping with his stepmother.

He just laughed. "Not yet." If I didn't know him so well, I would think he was joking. Sadly, he was probably very serious. "How's Reese liking the job?" he asked, jumping down from the fence. Maybe that meant he was about to leave me in peace.

"She loves it. Piper's been good to her."

"Good to know I won't have to kick anyone's ass, then," he said with a smirk.

I didn't even acknowledge him. He loved to try to make me mad. "Go to work," I told him.

"Not time yet," he replied.

"Go in early."

I was going to buy a ring tomorrow, or at least look for one that I wanted to see on Reese's hand. I couldn't picture what that would be, exactly, but it had to be perfect. It had to be Reese.

While I worked all day, I thought of different ways to propose. I wanted to make it something special that she'd never forget and that she could share over and over again. She deserved the best. I was going to give that to her. For the rest of my life.

Those thoughts got me through the day and kept me from

missing her too much. I looked forward to picking her up every day. I checked the clock as it got closer to five, growing more anxious with every minute.

When I opened her office door, her bottom was up in the air as she bent down over a low drawer of a file cabinet. The jeans she wore fit like a second skin.

"Don't move," I said, walking up behind her and sliding my hands over her plump bottom.

She tilted her head to the side and looked up at me with a giggle. "Well, hello to you, too."

"My girl has a fine ass," I replied, caressing it while she remained bent over for me.

"Thank you, but if I stay in this position, I'm going to get a cramp."

I took my hands off her bottom and stepped back reluctantly. When she stood up, I reached for her hips and pulled her backside up against my front. "Mmmm," I murmured in her ear. "Missed you."

She melted back into me. "Missed you, too."

I slid my hands up the front of her shirt and cupped both of her breasts, letting their heaviness fill my hands.

She laid her head back against my chest and made a soft moaning sound that only encouraged me more. With a tug, I pulled down the lace cups of her bra and rolled each nipple between my fingers. "Feels so good," I whispered in her ear before kissing her temple.

"I couldn't agree more," she said breathlessly.

Having her go all butter-soft and willing on me was hard on my self-control. I was already imagining bending her over the desk and taking us both to a happy place. I started to slide my hands down, but she grabbed them and held them there.

"Don't," she said, pressing her chest further into my hands. "I need this job."

I needed *her*, but this could be done in my truck if we couldn't make it home.

"I want to pull off these tight jeans and sink inside you, baby. We need to leave. *Now*."

Her hands went to her waist, and she started unbuttoning her jeans. What the hell? Reese liked having sex, but she was never one to initiate it in a public place like this, where someone could walk in. Including her boss.

"Piper left for a business meeting with Arthur. No one's here," she said as she shoved her jeans down and wiggled her hips. Her jeans fell to her ankles, and then she placed both of her hands on the edge of the desk, throwing her hair over her shoulder and looking back at me. "I need you now."

This wasn't like her, but I wasn't going to complain. Her sweet ass was wiggling and waiting. No way in hell was I telling her no. If someone walked in, I'd cover her up; I couldn't give a shit if they saw my ass.

She spread her legs as far as her jeans would let her and stuck her bottom up high in the air. This wasn't a sight a man could turn down. It was beauty and sex all rolled into one.

I quickly undid my jeans and shoved them down before sliding my hands back up her shirt and grabbing her breasts, now swaying freely as she bent over. "Are you wet?" I asked her, pressing a kiss to her back.

"My panties are soaked."

Fuck.

I used one hand to position myself, then sank in with one swift thrust. She cried out and bucked beneath me. Her breasts filled my hands as I began sliding in and out slowly, enjoying her tight heat and soft moans.

I kissed every spot on her back and neck that I could reach while my hands went to work pleasing her nipples.

"Mase," she panted. "Oh, God."

Not gonna lie; I loved it when she called me God. "My hot, sweet pussy," I replied as I worked my way in and out of her.

Soon she'd have a ring on her finger telling the world she was mine. The thought of that made my inner caveman roar to life and my dick pulse harder inside her. I wanted to claim her. Mark her and make sure no one else ever touched her.

"Yes," she moaned. "Harder."

I began to pump inside her with more intensity, and her hands fisted against the desk as she cried my name. Her walls squeezed me, and I began to spasm and tighten as I released into her, her name on my lips.

It took several moments for both of us to catch our breath. When the world came back into view, I smiled as she lay across the desk, sated.

"I can't believe we did that," she said breathily.

"Honestly, me, neither. But I'm sure glad we did."

She laughed and buried her head in her hands. "Me, too."

My chest tightened with emotion, and I ran my fingertips down her back. She was my woman.

Reese

The next few days went by without me having to deal with Captain. It had been a reckless move to have sex in my office, but I needed to associate the place with Mase. The next time Captain put food on this desk, I'd know it was right where Mase had taken me. It felt like our spot now. In my mind, it cleared all the Captain out of here. I could even smell Mase now when I walked in. He had marked this area, and I liked that feeling. It gave me confidence. It felt like he was here with me.

There was no sign of Captain on Friday, and I breathed a sigh of relief at the end of the work week. No more lunches, no more comments meant to make me question Mase, no more flirting. I could enjoy my job without his annoying presence.

Mase and I had just arrived home when Major pulled up, dressed in a pair of jeans, a fitted black T-shirt, boots, and a cowboy hat on his head. "When y'all ready to head out?" he asked, as if we had plans.

I glanced up at Mase, who was scowling. "I told you we weren't going with you."

Major didn't let that get to him. "But I got three tickets to hear Pat Green at Billy Bob's tonight," he said, holding up the tickets. "You can't make me go alone. Besides, it's Pat Green. Get your asses dressed, and let's go."

I had no idea who Pat Green was, but I could tell by the look on Mase's face that he did. He seemed to be contemplating it. I waited, and then he turned to look at me. "You up for a concert tonight? Or would you rather stay here?"

I could tell he wanted to go, and honestly, it sounded like fun. I didn't know what Billy Bob's was or who Pat Green was, but I was up for anything. I nodded. "Yep. I like concerts." I had actually never been to a concert, but I didn't mention that.

"And you'll fucking love Pat Green. Ain't nothing better than him in concert except Robert Earl Keen. Wish like hell he'd been playing tonight. But that's for another time. Go get your sexy ass fixed up," Major said, which drew a scowl from Mase.

Major just chuckled and sauntered past us into the house.

"Once you get over his dumb-ass shit, he's tolerable," Mase said, still sounding annoyed.

I laughed. I liked Major. He was funny. "He doesn't bother me."

Mase didn't look convinced as we headed to the bedroom to get ready.

"No fuckdickery in there. We got a show to get to. Besides, it ain't fair for me to have to listen and not get to watch," Major called out behind us.

We ate delicious barbecue at the café at Billy Bob's before finding our seats. I didn't have cowgirl gear to match the two cowboys I was with, but I did have on my boots and jeans. I had tied up a flannel shirt the way I'd seen Piper do to reveal my midriff, but Mase had untied it, shaking his head, and tucked it back in for me.

This place wasn't what I pictured a honky-tonk would look like, and I'd said as much when we drove up. Mase told me it wasn't a true honky-tonk; it was a big building with a restaurant, a store, and a huge stage. I couldn't take in everything fast enough, though I quickly realized I was in the minority without a cowgirl hat.

Once we found our seats, Mase took the one between Major and me. There were two empty seats beside me, but the rest of the row was filling up fast. After Mase and Major left to get beers for themselves and a soda for me, I settled down and watched the people as they arrived. Several girls had their shirts tied like I'd tried to do mine. Smiling, I thought of Mase's possessive streak; I liked that he didn't want to show me off.

Someone slipped into the seat beside me, and I glanced up to see familiar green eyes and that stupid smirk. What the heck? He apparently read my face easily, because his smirk turned into a grin. "Fancy meeting you here," he drawled, as if he didn't have a hand in this somehow.

A woman with curly blond hair and an overly bright smile leaned over him, showing me her impressive cleavage in the shiny silver tank top she was wearing. "Hi, I'm Kinsley," she said as she placed a hand on Captain's leg. I felt like sighing in relief that he had a date. I wished he'd let Kinsley sit by me instead.

"Nice to meet you. I'm Reese," I replied, with a smile that I didn't have to force. It was very nice to meet her. Nicer than she could possibly know.

"Isn't Reese a boy's name?" she asked with a giggle. "I mean, I've never heard a girl called that before."

I decided not to point out that Reese Witherspoon was a famous actress. I just shrugged. "Well, you have now," I replied and went back to looking at the people around me and hoping that was the end of this conversation with either of them.

"Didn't know you were a Pat Green fan," Captain said beside me. I shot him a quick smile that I didn't feel.

"I have no idea who he is. But Mase likes him, so here we are."

Captain made a *tsk*ing sound. "A man should take his woman where *she* wants to go."

I fisted my hands in my lap. He was already starting in on me. "He does. I wanted to come tonight. I like music, and I've never been to a concert before."

He didn't say anything at first, but my luck ran out. "So this is your first concert? Ever?" His tone was disbelieving.

I nodded but didn't look at him.

Kinsley asked him something that I couldn't hear, and as she chatted away, I knew she was fighting to keep his attention. I couldn't be more thankful for her. If Mase and Major would hurry up with the drinks, then I'd have Mase to lean into and feel safe from Captain's nonstop badgering.

"Pat Green is a grassroots kind of country. He's Texas country. I think you'll enjoy him," Captain said to me. "He puts on a good show."

I turned to look at him. "Out of all the seats in this huge arena, how did you end up in the one right beside me?" I asked. This wasn't just coincidental.

Captain looked smug. "Where do you think Major got the tickets from?" he drawled.

I knew it. Dang that man.

"If I'd known you had never been to a concert before, I'd have opted for something bigger, though," he said.

I let his comment sink in. What was he getting at? It wasn't like he had gotten these tickets for the sole purpose of getting me here. He didn't even know who Major was going to invite. Or did he?

I had started to ask him when I spotted Mase's hat, followed by his long, muscular body clad in blue jeans, walking toward me. He was mine—this man who made women's heads turn regularly. It was hard to believe it, but he was.

"Sorry it took me so long. The line was bad," he said, sinking down beside me and handing me the soda I had requested. He hadn't noticed Captain yet.

But Major had. He held up a hand and grinned. "Hey, River, Kinsley. Great seats, man. Thanks!"

Mase tensed beside me, then turned his head to see Captain and his date before looking back at me. I leaned into him and smiled to assure him that everything was fine. He put his arm around my shoulders, and I leaned closer to him, which seemed to ease his tension.

"River gave me the tickets. Kinsley's the head waitress at the restaurant. They hooked up recently," I heard Major tell Mase.

Mase just nodded. I knew he wasn't a fan of the idea of being at a concert paid for by Captain. He ran his fingertips over my arm, tracing patterns while he held me close. His eyes remained on the empty stage, and I knew he was thinking hard.

Captain got up and headed down the stairs—for drinks, I figured. I smiled at Mase. "I'm looking forward to this."

He pressed a kiss to my nose. "Me, too. One of his songs reminds me of you. Having you here while he sings it will be pretty damn perfect."

I liked knowing he thought of me when he heard a song. I took a sip of my soda and relaxed. We were going to enjoy ourselves. No need to let Captain ruin it. Besides, Mase didn't care for him because Captain had said a few rude comments. He didn't know everything. He'd get over Captain being there soon enough.

When the lights went down and the stage lit up, everyone stood up from their seats, hooting and hollering. Whistles and shouts of "Hell, yeah!" filled the place. Mase stood up, reached for my hand, and pulled me in front of him, wrapping his arms around me. I leaned back against his chest. Nothing else mattered.

I was wrapped up in Mase, and the music was great. Major sang along beside us, and I was surprised by how good he sounded. Like, really good. I never once looked over at Captain and Kinsley. They weren't even here as far as I was concerned.

Pat Green stood onstage and starting talking about a song, and everyone around me seemed to know what he was talking about, because the cheering began again. "This is it," Mase whispered in my ear. "My song to you."

That got my immediate attention. I stood taller and waited for the music to start again. Mase caressed my arms as he held me and pressed his mouth near my ear as he sang the words. Having him sing to me made me light-headed.

All I'm looking for is you.

The words made my heart flutter in my chest and I turned to look up at him.

You came upon me wave on wave.

He sang with such intensity in his eyes I clung to him tighter and prayed this moment would never end. Just us here, together, with Mase singing to me. It was a perfect night.

Mase

After dropping Reese off at work on Monday morning, I pulled up to the stables and saw a face I didn't expect. You could look at me and never guess my father was a rock legend, but you couldn't say the same for Rush Finlay. He had the look. Even though he had a three-year-old son now, he didn't look like a dad. I doubted he ever would.

But why the hell was he at my ranch? Getting out of the truck, I closed the door and headed toward him. He pushed his sunglasses up and smiled at me. "You always get to work this late?" he asked with a smirk.

"Had to take Reese to work. Didn't expect to get back and see you standing here."

He gave a small shrug. "Brought Blaire and Nate to visit with her brother. Figured I'd give them some family bonding time and come see how things were going here."

I'd almost forgotten that Captain was Blaire's brother. Remembering him sitting beside Reese at the concert this weekend still pissed me off.

"You look like you know Blaire's brother and would like to smash his face in," Rush said with an amused laugh.

"He works with someone I do business with. He's made a few comments I wasn't crazy about concerning Reese."

"Sounds like Captain," Rush said. "He's just a smart-mouth. First time I met him, he pointed out that I'd gotten Blaire pregnant before marrying her and that it was the backward way to do it. Pissed me the hell off. He's grown on me, though."

Maybe I was being too hard on him. It wasn't like he was sniffing around Reese. I was just being touchy and possessive; the vibe I was getting from him when he was around Reese could possibly just be me overthinking things. "I'll keep that in mind," I replied. "So you come to help me mend some fences?" I knew good and well that Rush Finlay wasn't here to do any hard labor.

"I'll pass on that offer. I was checking to see if Harlow has talked to you about Kiro lately."

Huh? I shook my head.

Rush sighed and nodded like he'd expected that. "Harlow's mom isn't doing so well, and he's not dealing with it. He's falling apart. Dad said they wouldn't let him near her for three days because the medicine she was on lowered her immune system. Kiro got so hammered that Dad had to throw him into a shower to get the vomit off him before putting him to bed. He wakes up and starts drinking right away. He yells at everyone. The only person he's talking to is Harlow. She's worried about him. Thought you might want to know about it."

Shit. Motherfucking shit! Harlow didn't need this. And why hadn't she called me? I threw the feed I'd carried over from my truck against the wall and swore loudly.

"Dad said we don't get it. We don't know how Kiro was

back when he had Emily. He told me it would be like me losing Blaire. And man, I can't imagine that. If Kiro loves Emily like I love Blaire, then, dude, he's in fucking pain and has been for twenty-three years."

I understood that Kiro loved Emily. It was obvious. But dammit, he had a daughter with a heart problem. One year ago, Harlow had been given a miracle when she gave birth to Lila Kate and lived through the process. She didn't need this shit on her now. He never thought of anyone else, only how much he was hurting.

"Harlow can't deal with this," I said angrily. My brain was already spinning. I had to do something. I couldn't leave her to deal alone. I also needed to see Kiro. This shit had to stop. One day, Emily would pass away. She'd been given much longer than any doctor expected. Kiro had to come to grips with that.

Rush nodded. "She has Grant. He's worried like hell about her. She's crying a lot. I figured you needed to know. Harlow needs you. She needs you to do something with your father."

He was right. She did. "Thanks for telling me. Don't know why she hasn't called me." Or Grant, which pissed me off. Grant should have called me.

"She said you'd get mad at Kiro and it wouldn't help anything. She asked Grant not to call you, so Grant came to me instead. She never asked him not to tell me to tell you."

Damn. I had to give my brother-in-law more credit. "I need to pack and let Momma and Dad know I'm leaving. Shit! Reese has a new job. She's not gonna want to take time off yet, and honestly, I don't want her seeing all this shit with Kiro. It's fucked-up. She doesn't need to be involved."

"Go on and figure things out. We'll be flying out at six tonight if you want to leave with us. We've got the jet."

"Thanks. I'll see you then."

"Life as a rocker's son sucks more than it doesn't," Rush said, and he headed up the hill to leave.

I could have said he understood, but he didn't really. He was the son of Dean Finlay. Dean had never done the shit Kiro had done. Dean had been a loving, present father—for the most part. Dean wasn't always mixed up in some crazy shit. Rush had no idea how it felt to be Kiro Manning's son.

It sucked. That's what it fucking did. It sucked. All the time.

Reese

When the office door opened just after two, I somehow knew it was going to be him. My entire body tensed as I looked up to meet Captain's eyes. There was a gleam in them as he sauntered into the room.

"Good afternoon, Reese. I have some paperwork and receipts for you," he said, as he sank down into the leather chair closest to my desk.

"OK," I replied simply. I'd already resigned myself not to ask him about the concert tickets.

"You looked like you enjoyed the concert," he said, as if he had read my mind. Again. How did he do that?

"It was a great concert," I said. Although I had nothing to compare it with.

He smirked. "You say that now. Wait until you see a band like U2 in concert. Then you'll know what a great concert is."

I didn't even know who U2 was, so I just ignored his remark. "The paperwork?" I asked, holding out my hand, wanting to get this over with.

He chuckled. "You don't like me, Reese. Why is that?"

I didn't have an answer, other than that he made me nervous. And he flirted with me. Well, I guess that was the answer. "You flirt. I don't like it," I replied.

He studied me for a moment, and then his amused smile turned to something more serious as he leaned forward, placing his elbows on his knees. His face was closer to me, and the table between us felt like a safety guard.

"I haven't been flirting with you, Reese. When I flirt with you, you'll know it."

Oh. OK. Well, what he was doing now seemed kind of flirty. But was I wrong about that? Was I assuming that his trying to be friendly was flirting? No. He had made comments about wanting what Mase had.

"You've made comments, comments about me . . ." I trailed off, feeling my face grow hot.

He shrugged. "I'm honest. I don't worry about what others think. If I want to say something, I do. Doesn't mean I was flirting, baby."

He was so confusing. I fisted my hand in my lap, totally frustrated. "OK. Well, then, let's forget all this and get to business. What do you have for me?"

He reached into his back pocket and pulled out a manila folder. "Here you go." Then he stood up and headed for the door. "If you have questions, you can call or text," he said, without looking back at me. When the door closed behind him, I sank back into my seat and let out a frustrated sigh. How had I ended up sounding like the jerk? He had been honest and turned it around to make me look like the idiot.

Shaking him off, I opened the folder to find more paperwork and receipts than I was going to have time to handle today. I still had several things to do for Piper. She would be gone tomorrow, and I had to feed and water the horses, on top of brushing them down and cleaning stalls. Piper had recently let her stable help go because the girl had kept talking on her phone during business hours. She hadn't hired a replacement yet.

I had a busy few days ahead of me and needed to work late that night. I had pulled out my phone from my pocket and started to dial Mase when his name lit up my screen.

Smiling, I answered, ready to hear his voice. "Hey, I was just about to call you."

"Hey, baby, I've got a problem. I hate to have to call you about this, but I'm packing up now and have to nail some things down before I fly out at six."

What? Packing? "What's wrong?" I asked, not liking the idea of him going anywhere on such short notice.

"It's Kiro. Harlow's mom is having health complications, and Kiro isn't dealing with it well. He's acting out like he always does, and Harlow has been dealing with it on her own. She doesn't need this shit. Her heart . . . well, I've told you about her heart. I just need to handle him. Get him calm and reassure my sister that everything is going to be OK. I'd take you, but this is going to be ugly. Kiro . . . isn't normal. He's a crazy fuck. But I don't want to leave you, either. I'm having a hard time with this."

I couldn't leave. I had more work than I could handle as it was, plus Piper was going out of town and was relying on me. "I have to work anyway. Piper is leaving, and I have to cover for her. Just go. Help Kiro, and keep me updated."

"I love you. I'm going to miss you. I'll call every night.

Momma said she'd give you a ride to and from work, and she'll pick you up at five tonight; I have to leave for the airport before then."

"I love you, too. I'll be fine. I'll miss you, but your family needs you. Do you think there's any way Maryann can come get me at six thirty instead? I have to work late tonight."

He hesitated. "Yeah, she can. I just hate the idea of you working that late."

I wanted to hug him tight and feel his kiss on my lips. My heart hurt already from missing him. But I wouldn't let him know that. He had enough to deal with right now. I wasn't adding more to it. "I'll be fine. I just have a lot of paperwork that needs to be filed first. Travel safe, and call me when you get there."

He sighed. "God, I hate leaving you."

I hated it, too. "It won't be too long. I'll miss you, but I'll be here when you're back."

"I love you. So damn much," he said fervently.

"I love you more," I replied.

Mase

We took the private jet to Florida so I could check on Harlow, but I wasn't staying with her long. I had to get to Los Angeles and deal with Kiro. I just had to talk to Harlow first; she knew what all was going on. I also wanted to assure her that I would handle the situation right. Anything to keep her from worrying.

Grant opened the door before I even knocked. I'd texted him that I was on my way from the airport. He looked stressed. "Thanks for coming," he said in a whisper.

I nodded. "Get in touch with me sooner next time, yeah?"

Grant nodded his head toward the back of the house. "She's out on the back porch. She's calling Dean to check on Kiro. Lila Kate is already in bed."

I dropped my duffel bag onto the floor and headed back to the porch.

I saw Harlow sitting in a chair with her phone in her hand, dangling at her side. Her chin rested on her knees. "He didn't answer," she said, sounding sad. She still hadn't looked at me. She thought I was Grant.

"I'm headed out there later tonight. I'll find out how he is and call you right away," I said.

At the sound of my voice, her head jerked up, and she turned to look at me. Immediately, her eyes filled with tears. "I told him not to tell you," she said with a choked voice.

"He didn't. Rush did. *You* should have," I said, walking over to her, reaching for one of her small hands, and holding it in mine.

"You'll be mad at him. He doesn't need that. He's hurting," she said with a sob.

I knew that. And if it wasn't for Harlow, I'd go beat his ass for acting like this. But I wouldn't hurt my sister in any way. "I won't do that. I know he's hurting. I'm going to talk to him. See if I can't get him to see things clearer and lay off the vodka. He's got to find another way to cope without turning to alcohol. Next, he'll be back on drugs. Someone has to stop him, and we both know Dean can't."

Harlow dropped her forehead to her knees. "He loves her so much. I can't imagine that, Mase. I can't comprehend how he deals with seeing the woman he loves so much lost in her own body. It breaks my heart. I want him to find a way to be happy again. He hasn't been happy in so long."

If any of Kiro Manning's kids were going to cry over him, it would be Harlow. She loved him in a way I didn't understand. The father she knew was so different from the Kiro I was familiar with. I was thankful that he cherished Harlow. I'd hate him and completely wash my hands of the man if he didn't adore Harlow the way he did. That was his one redeeming quality in my eyes. He loved my little sister. That was enough for me to try to stop him from killing himself with his own stupidity. "He has held on to Emily for a long time. This is rocking him. He feels like he's losing her again. But he's going to lose himself if someone doesn't shake some sense into him. I won't be mean to him, but I will force him to see the big picture. He needs that, Harlow."

She sniffled and nodded as she wiped at a stray tear that rolled down her face. "I love him," she said softly.

I reached over and pulled her into a tight hug. "I know you do. And because you do, I'll do everything I can to save him from himself."

She clung to me, and we sat there like that until her quiet sobs died down. When she pulled back, she used her sleeve to clean her tear-streaked face. "Where's Reese?"

Reese. I'd had to leave Reese. I hated leaving Reese behind. I needed her. "She has a new job, and her boss isn't going to be there tomorrow. She has to fill in for her. And honestly, I don't want Reese to be there to see Kiro in his current state."

Harlow gave me a sad smile. "I'm sorry you had to leave her."

I was, too. I reached out and tucked a stray hair behind Harlow's ear. "I miss her. I won't lie. But right now, Kiro needs help. And for you, I'm going to make sure he gets it."

Harlow sighed and sank back into her seat. "He loves you, too, you know. He's proud of you. He doesn't say it, but he's proud of the man you became. That you're not like him."

I wasn't like him because I was raised by a good man. I didn't say that to Harlow, though. I just nodded, because that was what she needed.

She laughed and reached over to squeeze my hand. "You're agreeing with me because you don't want me upset. You're as bad as Grant. I know you don't believe it. I don't know if you ever will. But I know Daddy. I know he loves you."

I smiled at the sound of her laughter. That eased the tightness in my chest some. "I just want you to promise me you'll stop worrying. Don't cry. Rest, enjoy Lila Kate, and give poor Grant a break. The man is worried sick over you."

Harlow glanced back at the house, and a sweet smile touched her lips. "I got lucky with him. He's wonderful. He makes everything in my world brighter."

Good. "Focus on that, then. The bright shit Grant creates. Just stop worrying."

Harlow laughed again, and I felt much better about her. I could leave her and deal with Kiro now, knowing she was better and her mind was at ease.

The door opened, and Grant stuck his head out. "Did I hear her laugh?" he asked in a hopeful tone.

"Yes, you did. I bring the magic, man. You could take lessons from me," I said, standing up. I walked over and pressed a kiss on top of Harlow's head. "Love you."

She squeezed my arm. "Love you, too."

Grant walked over to her, and she stood up to cuddle against his chest. He began caressing her back and tucked her head under his chin. "Thank you," he said, looking at me like I'd just solved all the world's problems.

"Call me no matter what she says next time. No reason for her to worry. She's stubborn, but you can be more stubborn. I've seen it. I was there when you stood at a hospital door, refusing to move until your wife came out of that room alive."

A moment of fear and then relief flashed through his eyes at the memory. "Noted," he replied.

Harlow grinned at me. "You're teaching him to gang up on me."

I shrugged. "When it's about your health and happiness, little sis, I'll do whatever the hell I have to do. And so will he."

Harlow pressed a kiss to Grant's chin. He turned his attention back to her, and I was suddenly invisible. I had started to tell her I was leaving for Los Angeles when she turned to look at me. "You aren't leaving tonight. You're staying the night and seeing your niece in the morning. Then you're eating breakfast with us. I want some time with you before you take off to deal with Daddy."

I wanted to get back to Reese, but I was also exhausted, and she was right—I should see Lila Kate first. I nodded, and Grant chuckled. "What?" I asked him.

He smirked. "It's fun to see that she has you wrapped around her little finger, too."

I would deny that, but I loved Harlow, and it was hard to tell her no.

Besides, if I saw Kiro while I was exhausted, I wasn't going to do any good. I could make Harlow happy and be productive when I finally dealt with him.

Reese

Last night, the bed was lonely without Mase. I'd finally managed to get some sleep, but it wasn't enough. I'd woken up yawning. Before Maryann got there to pick me up, I fixed a large pot of coffee and put it in the thermos that Mase usually used.

I heard Maryann's truck pull up and quickly grabbed my lunch and the thermos. Running out to the truck, I realized it wasn't Mase's mom driving but Major. I opened the passenger-side door and stuck my head in. "Are you my ride?" I asked, making sure he hadn't just shown up looking for Mase.

His grin always looked like he was keeping a big secret. "Yep. Maryann had to help with some complications with a calf. She told me to give you a ride."

I climbed in and put my things down on the seat beside me before buckling up. "Thank you," I told him.

"You're welcome. But I'll be completely honest here. She promised me biscuits and gravy, so . . ."

I laughed. Mase was always complaining because Major ate all of his momma's food. From what I'd heard, Major didn't have much of a mom, so I kind of felt sorry for him. But then again, he had slept with his last stepmother. Maybe he didn't deserve my sympathy.

"Talked to Mase?"

"Yes. He called last night when he landed in Florida to let me know he was going to see Harlow."

Major let out a long sigh. "That family is wack."

Mase was a celebrity's kid. Life wasn't supposed to be normal. But apparently, it was worse than I had realized. "He seems worried," I said simply.

Major glanced over at me before he pulled out onto the main road. "He *is* worried. But he's only worried about Harlow. If it wasn't for Harlow, he wouldn't give a shit about Kiro. That man may have given him life, but he's not Mase's dad."

I had to agree, though it made me sad to think that he didn't have a relationship with his real father the way Harlow did. Kiro had missed out on knowing this wonderful man he'd helped create.

"So how's the job going? Liking it? Ready to quit?"

I opened my thermos and yawned. "I like it. Piper's really great to work for."

He nodded. "That's good. Sucks you couldn't go with Mase, though."

Yes, it did suck.

"You reckon he's gonna pop the question soon?"

Pop the question? Huh? I frowned and put my thermos down. "What question?" I asked.

Major looked at me like I was joking. Then he laughed and held up his left hand. " 'Will you marry me?' That kinda question."

Oh . . . Oh! I hadn't thought of that yet. Sure, I was planning on my future with Mase, but this wasn't something

I was expecting anytime soon. We had just started living together.

My silence made Major chuckle. "Guess not," he replied.

I looked over at him, wondering what he expected me to say. Luckily, he was pulling up to the Stouts' ranch, and I could end this conversation soon. Once he drove up to the stables, I'd be free. I had no answer for him other than that I doubted it.

When his truck came to a stop, he turned to me. "Just out of curiosity, is that silence because you don't want him to ask you that question or because you think he doesn't want to ask?"

I decided to take a page from Captain's book and be honest. "I think he isn't ready. We're still kind of new. If he was really ready to marry me now, he would have asked already. I think he wants to wait until we've been together for a while."

Major nodded and then shrugged. "Maybe," he said, then tipped the front of his cowboy hat at me, much the same way Mase often did. "Have a good day, Reese."

I got out of the truck fast before Major could think of any more nosy questions.

Two hours into work, I had drunk my entire thermos of coffee and was working on a new cup from the coffee pot in the office. I was kneeling on the floor, looking for a file that Piper had called for, when the door to my office opened, and in walked Captain.

I was not going to be rude today. He had said he wasn't flirting with me, so I wasn't going to be so defensive. We would be working together for a while, and I needed to find a way to do that without feeling I needed to keep my guard up. Besides, I wasn't normally a rude person. It was hard to do.

In light of my new attitude, I gave him a smile. "Good morning," I said. I could see the surprise on his face. I wasn't going to let him say something "honest" and mess this up. "I've got to look for a file for Piper, then I'll help you with whatever you need." I went back to hunting for the file.

"Did I walk into the wrong office?" Captain asked.

I knew he was going to say something. He had to. It was the way he was. I flashed him another friendly smile. "Nope. Just trying to make this easier. I have no reason to be defensive with you if you're not flirting with me."

Finally, the file appeared, and I grabbed it. I stood up and dusted off my jeans before walking back behind my desk. "More paperwork for me to file?" I asked.

He tilted his head and studied me. Well, crap. This was supposed to be easy, but he was going to make a big deal out of it. "Not today. I actually need to see a receipt I brought you last week. If you'll point me to the right cabinet, I'll dig through to find it."

I nodded. "OK. The second drawer has files labeled with the dates on the receipts."

He was still looking at me like he wasn't sure what to do with me. Finally, he nodded and walked over to find his receipt. I took that as my opportunity to sit down and find the information that I needed to text Piper. I pulled out my phone and took several pictures of the paperwork she needed. Then I sent them to her in a text.

It was time to return voice mails about lessons, but Captain was still in my office, which seemed awkward. Besides, if he was watching me, I wouldn't be able to write without messing up.

I decided to get another cup of coffee, even though I was getting jittery from all the caffeine. I had to get better sleep tonight. Maybe I could sleep with one of Mase's shirts. If I smelled him, it might help.

"Found it," Captain said, standing up with a paper in his hand. "Thanks. That's very organized."

I nodded. I was proud of that. Before Mase, I never would have been able to file anything according to its date. He had changed that.

Captain walked over and kept his gaze on me. "There were a couple of dates that were a little mixed up. I fixed them. I'm sure staring at numbers that much gets to your eyes after a while."

Crap. I felt my face heat up. Here I was feeling so accomplished, when I'd messed up some receipts. Of all the people to notice, it had to be Captain.

"No need to look like you did something unforgivable. It was just a couple of receipts."

My face only flushed more. I wanted him to leave. I needed a moment to regroup. Then I was going to check all the files. I didn't want Piper to see them and think I couldn't do this job. I was proud of this job. I was good at it. Or, at least, I'd thought I was.

"Reese, look at me." Captain's voice sounded commanding, and my head jerked up to meet his gaze. "You look like you're about to cry. Fuck, if I'd known it was gonna upset you like that, I wouldn't have told you about the few receipts I found. It was an honest mistake."

My eyes stung with tears, and I hated that. I didn't want to feel weak or damaged. I also didn't want Captain to see my weakness.

"Swear to God, if you cry over this, I'm going to be pissed. Why are you so upset?"

Maybe it was exhaustion coupled with all the caffeine I'd poured into myself, but I was definitely emotional. I was also missing Mase. He was my security blanket, and with him gone, I had to be strong. I had always been strong before I met Mase. Why was I falling apart now?

"Reese—"

"I'm dyslexic," I blurted out.

He went still for a moment, and then regret flashed in his eyes, and for the first time ever, I saw Captain look apologetic. I didn't want sympathy, though.

"I'm learning how to work around it, and I've come a long way. I just hate making mistakes like that. It reminds me of where I was before. I don't want to feel like that again." I prepared myself for Captain's apology and gritted my teeth. I didn't want to hear it, but I knew it was coming.

"Lock up, and come with me. There's someone I want you to meet," he said, as if I would do exactly as he told me.

I shook my head. "I have to work."

He frowned. "Fine. After work, then."

I wasn't going anywhere with Captain. "I can't."

"Because of Mase." It wasn't a question. He was just stating a fact. "Then I'll bring him to you."

Who? I had started to ask when Captain turned and walked to the door to leave.

He glanced back. "I don't want you to ever cry again over

that. You should only be proud of what you've accomplished. Hell, that's an honest mistake anyone could have made. Don't let your weakness define you, Reese. Ever. Your strengths should define you."

Then he was gone.

Mase

Dean Finlay opened the door to the mansion he shared with Kiro in Beverly Hills. "He's already passed out for the night. I've had a room prepared for you," he said when I walked inside. "He'll be a mean bastard in the morning. It's his new routine."

I wasn't scared of the old man's temper. "I'll handle him. This shit has to stop. He's so damn selfish," I said, angry that he was making life hell not only for Harlow but also for Dean, his best friend. Other than Harlow, Dean was the only person who loved the man.

"You don't know what she was to him. Unless you lived through it with them, you can't understand, Mase. He was a different man because of her. The accident, it created someone none of us recognized. It shattered his soul. When that happens to you, you never come back from that."

I was tired of hearing how losing Emily gave him the right to be a world-class asshole. "You know this because you've had that kind of love? 'Cause you sure as hell don't act like him."

Dean sighed heavily and shook his head. "Never been in love like that. After seeing how it changed Kiro when he lost her, I never let anyone get close enough to me. I wasn't going to ever know that pain. Don't want it."

I wasn't sure which was worse, loving and losing or not ever knowing that kind of love at all. Life without Reese seemed empty, devoid, pointless. Would I become like my father if I lost her? I wanted to believe I wouldn't, but I wasn't sure a man without a soul could be anything else. If that was true, then could I forgive the man? Could I understand him and not hate him for what he was doing to my sister? Had she already made this connection? She had not only Grant but Lila Kate, too. I didn't want to think of her losing either of them.

"Don't judge him when you haven't been there," Dean said, with a slap on my back. "Now, go get some rest. You're gonna need it. He won't be thrilled to see you."

He was right. Kiro was going to be pissed that I was here to deal with him. He didn't want dealing with. He wanted to wallow in his pain. But when I faced him tomorrow, I knew I was going to see him differently. I had to remind myself that this would be me if I lost Reese. A world without her in it was incomprehensible.

I'd set my alarm to wake me up at nine so I could be dressed and ready to face my father. I would need coffee before I did this. Yesterday, Harlow had kept finding reasons to keep me in Rosemary Beach. Finally, I had told her I loved her but I had to go. Getting home to Reese was important, and I had to get to Kiro before I could go home to Reese.

Heading to the kitchen, I heard two voices. I recognized Dean but not the female he was with; she had an accent. Stepping into the bright room, I saw an older lady working over the stove while Dean sat at the table, drinking coffee and leafing through an issue of *Rolling Stone* magazine. He glanced up and smiled at me.

"Good morning, sunshine. You got up before him. Thank fuck," he said.

"Coffee?" I asked.

The lady wiped her hands on her apron and started to hurry over to the coffee pot.

"I got it," I told her. "Just point me to the cups."

She gave me a nervous smile, then glanced over at Dean.

"Marlana is new," he said. "Marlana, this is Kiro's son. You don't have to wait on him. He's nothing like his father."

She glanced up at me, still looking nervous, then reached into the cabinet and got me a cup before hurrying back to her skillet on the stove. Poor woman had to deal with my crazy-ass father. No wonder she was a nervous mess.

I poured my coffee and walked over to the table to sit across from Dean.

"You want a newspaper? I think there's one over by the front door. Marlana normally gets it and puts it there. Don't know why we have one, since neither of us reads it."

"I get it," Marlana said, turning around and hurrying out of the room. I didn't need the paper, but she was fast.

Dean shrugged. "She's very eager to please. If Kiro doesn't scare her off first."

"My plan is to make sure his head is on right before I leave here."

"Plans don't always pan out. Remember, that man lives and breathes for that woman. He's really losing her this time."

My chest ached. All I could think of was losing Reese.

"Makes you regret falling in love, eh?" Dean said, looking back down at the magazine in his hand.

He was wrong. I'd never regret Reese. I would never regret those feelings. She had opened up my world in a way I had never imagined. She had changed my life. She had given me true happiness. I shook my head. "No, it doesn't."

Dean looked back up at me.

"Before Reese, I didn't know that the world could be full of dreams. That you could wake up every day excited to breathe. That one smile from her could make me feel like a fucking king. Loving her is worth . . . it's worth it all. Living in fear of love isn't living."

He frowned and put his magazine down, then continued sipping his coffee. He didn't look like he believed me. In reality, he was as sad as Kiro. He didn't know true, raw emotion. He didn't know that one woman could make you feel everything.

I could tell he was thinking of saying something, but he changed his mind.

"Kiro won't crawl out of bed for another two hours. I suggest you let him get up on his own. If you wake him, you're just going to have a more difficult time."

"Fine. I'll eat and then call Reese."

Dean set his cup down. "Marlana is making pancakes and sausage. Or she was, until she ran off to get your paper. At least look at the damn thing. The woman is too old to be running around so much."

That was all he said before he walked out of the kitchen with a swagger that was similar to my father's. I decided a long time ago that only rock stars knew how to walk that way.

Marlana came shuffling in and put the paper in front of me. "Breakfast ready soon," she assured me, then went back to the stove.

I opened the paper, not giving a shit what it had to say, but, like Dean said, she'd gone and gotten it for me. I didn't want to hurt her feelings.

Reese

I had called and gotten Maryann to pick me up an hour early yesterday so I wouldn't be there when Captain returned. The more I thought about it, the more I wished I hadn't told him about my dyslexia. What was it about him that made me blurt stuff out?

Mase had called me when he landed in Los Angeles. We talked during his ride to his father's house in Beverly Hills. I could tell he was tense and nervous about what he was going to find when he got there, and I felt guilty about not being there with him.

To make up for leaving work early yesterday, I had come in early this morning. I had slept better than the night before because I was so tired from lack of sleep. If all went well today, Mase would be coming home.

Piper would also be back today, and I wanted to make sure everything was neat and ready for her. I checked on the horses and swept the floors of the dust that had blown in overnight. Then I headed back to my office.

The rest of the morning went quickly. I kept waiting for a call from Mase, but I focused on getting all my work done in case anything new came up today.

Right after Piper left for lunch, the door opened, and in walked a little boy who couldn't have been more than ten. At first, I thought he was a student of Piper's whose parents had gotten the time wrong. Until Captain walked in behind the kid.

What?

"Glad you're here. Henry and I made the drive out yesterday to find you'd already gone home. Early."

He had planned on bringing a kid to see me? I was confused. "Um, yes, I finished up early," which was a lie. I felt a twinge of guilt.

"That's all right. Henry and I made plans to come back here today. We even brought steak fajitas from the restaurant. Henry's dad is the head cook at Stouts and Hawkins here in Dallas. He's become my bud. I wanted to introduce him to one of my other friends."

What was he doing? Bringing me food again and using a kid so that I would eat with him and be nice? Captain made no sense. He said he wasn't flirting with me, but then he did things like this.

"My daddy makes the best steak fajitas," Henry said proudly. He was a cute kid. "He made you special ones. With his secret sauce."

"Oh, thank you. It smells delicious," I said to Henry as Captain began laying the food out in front of me.

"Can we have a picnic? It's more fun to eat outside. Besides, this place smells like horse poop," Henry said, looking up at Captain and crinkling his nose.

Captain laughed and brought his gaze to mine. "Would you be OK with that, Reese?"

Like I was going to tell this kid no. He knew that. Dang him. "Of course," I said through clenched teeth, then forced a smile as I picked up the box Captain had put in front of me.

"Great. I'll grab the blanket out of the back of my truck," Captain said. He headed out to his truck, leaving Henry and me with our hands full of food.

"He has a blanket in his truck?" I asked.

Henry nodded. "Yep. We look at stars on nights my daddy has to work too late."

So Captain watched a little boy while his daddy worked. Not what I was expecting. That didn't go with the image of Captain in my head.

"Kinsley went with us the other night. She was off work, and we got milkshakes and went to see the stars. But Kinsley didn't like it much. She griped a lot."

That didn't say a lot about her character. I hoped Captain wouldn't force her to be around Henry anymore. He didn't need that. I wondered where Henry's mother was, but it didn't sound like she was around, so I didn't ask.

"Got it. Lead the way, Henry. Take us to a prime picnic spot," Captain said, grinning at the boy. I had never seen that grin on him before. It was real. It wasn't calculated or planned. It wasn't a bad smile.

Henry walked a short way from the stables and stopped where I assumed he couldn't smell the horses anymore. He nodded his head to let us know we should settle here, his shaggy brown hair falling into his eyes. I wanted to tuck it behind his ear, but I was sure he wouldn't appreciate it.

Captain spread the blanket out for us, took the food from me, and placed it on the blanket while Henry laid out the food he had been carrying. Captain reached into his back pocket and tossed Henry a can of soda. Then he looked at me. "Got you one, too."

He handed me the can, and I managed a "Thank you." I sat with my legs crossed and placed the box of food he handed me in my lap.

"Ain't gonna be easy eating fajitas out here. But it don't stink, and it's more fun," Henry said, smiling at me.

"You're right. It does smell better, and it's a lot more fun. Besides, I eat in my office every day. This is a nice change."

Henry looked at Captain. "She's better than Kinsley. She knows what's fun," the boy said.

I didn't look at Captain. Instead, I focused on my food. I had to get through this lunch. I would set Captain straight when Henry wasn't with him. I didn't know what his motives were for bringing the child here. Was he trying to manipulate me?

I didn't trust him. This only justified that feeling.

I picked up my fajita and took a bite. I could see Henry's eyes on me, waiting for a reaction.

"Mmmm, this is amazing. The best fajita I've ever had. You're right, your daddy sure knows his stuff."

Henry beamed, then turned to his own food and began eating.

I could feel Captain watching me, but I wasn't going to look at him. I was going to eat this food and be nice to Henry, and then I was going to start locking my office door when Piper was out. No more Captain interruptions.

"Why don't you tell Reese about the book you're writing, Henry?" Captain said. I watched as Henry looked at him shyly, as if he was unsure. "She'll love it, promise," Captain encouraged him.

Henry finally turned his big brown eyes to me, and the freckles on his nose made his face even cuter. "Back in November, I won the spelling bee at my school. Then I went to a statewide spelling bee, and I won it, too. I'll be going to the nationals in May."

Wow. That was something to be proud of. At his age, I hadn't even been able to write my name correctly. "That's awesome!" I beamed at him. "You must be a very gifted speller."

Henry glanced at Captain again before looking at me. "That's why I'm writing a book. Because I'm dyslexic. That's when you don't always see words and numbers the way other people do," he said, watching me closely.

The reason Captain had wanted me to meet Henry was now becoming clear. This hadn't been some scheme. I nodded my head. "I know what dyslexia is," I assured him.

He seemed relieved that he didn't have to explain himself. "Lots of times, kids with dyslexia get ignored or believe they can't do something. I want to tell them they can. My daddy and I spelled words every minute we had a chance to for months before those spelling bees. I think people with dyslexia can do anything they want to. They just have to believe in themselves."

I felt emotion clog my throat. This little boy was going to live a full life. He'd never be told he was stupid, and he would have a chance to finish high school and get a college degree. I didn't know his father, but I loved him. I loved that Henry wasn't suffering what I had gone through. I put the unfinished fajita down and sniffled, trying not to cry. "That's a wonderful thing to do, Henry. Kids and adults with dyslexia need to hear that message. They need to be inspired by your story."

Henry was smiling from ear to ear now. "I think so, too. If it hadn't been for my dad telling me I could do anything over and over, I don't know if I'd have tried out for the spelling bee. But I wanted to, and he convinced me I could."

I wanted that for all kids. It was heartbreaking to know that not everyone would get that kind of support in their lives or be told that nothing was wrong with them. Knowing they were capable of so much would do wonders for their self-esteem. "Your dad sounds like a very special man," I said sincerely.

Henry nodded. "He is. He's the best."

Once again, no mention of his mother.

It was time for me to admit to Henry that I had dyslexia, too. Sharing this with people wasn't something I ever did. It was hard on me, but this little boy was going to share his story with the world. He was proud of what he could do while dealing with this challenge. There was no shame in being dyslexic.

"Henry," I said, and he looked up at me as he chewed his food. "I have dyslexia, too."

His little eyes went wide, and then a huge grin broke across his face. "I knew you were special," he replied. "Just like me."

Those words sank into my heart, and I knew they'd stay there forever.

Mase

It was well past lunchtime before Kiro came stumbling into the entertainment room, where I was sitting with Dean while he played on the Xbox. I had threatened to wake Kiro up several times, but each time, Dean shook his head and warned me I would just make things worse.

When Kiro's bleary, bloodshot eyes saw me, he stopped. "Fuck," he muttered, then walked toward the bar. That was my cue to stand up and do something.

"I'm here to talk, Kiro. I'd prefer to do that with you sober."

He tried to shove me aside, but he was too hungover and weak. I didn't budge. "My fucking house, boy. Move out of my way!" he yelled.

I didn't flinch. "Well, Harlow is my sister, and you upsetting her, stressing her out, and making her cry is my fucking business. So sit your sorry ass down and listen to me."

Just like I knew he would, he snapped out of his stupor at the sound of Harlow's name. "What's wrong with my baby girl?" he asked, running a hand through his hair, causing it to stick up even more.

"She's worried about you. She loves you. And you're upsetting her by acting this way. Think about her heart, Kiro. We

161

don't want something happening to her because you can't get your shit together."

He shook his head. "No, nothing can happen to my baby girl. I need her. Can't lose her," he said, sounding like a broken man instead of the angry drunk who had walked in here.

"Then snap out of this. Get your head on straight. Is this the way Emily would want you to behave? Would this make her happy?"

"Don't talk about my Emmy!" he roared, this time shoving me back with more force. "You don't understand what this is! You don't fucking understand. My heart." He stopped, tilted his head back, and looked up at the sky. "She stole my heart. That pretty angel face. So innocent and sweet. She'll always have it. My life with her was perfect." He turned his haunted gaze back to me. "Perfect! So fucking perfect! But it ended. I ended. And if I lose all I have left of her, I don't want to live anymore. I can't take this pain."

His eyes weren't those of the rock legend who appeared on the covers of magazines looking like he owned the world. He didn't have that swagger that defined him. Not now. He was shredded.

Kiro Manning was gone. In his place was a man who was about to become untethered from this earth. If he'd been a good father to me, if I loved him the way Harlow did, I wasn't sure I'd be able to stand here and take this. My chest tightened in pain for a man I had spent most of my life questioning if he gave a shit about me.

"Harlow needs you. Lila Kate needs a grandfather," I said simply, reminding him that if Emily was lost, his whole world wasn't gone. "If something happens to you, Harlow will be crushed. That girl adores you. Could you really do that to her? Can't you find the will to survive this and be the father she needs?"

Kiro stumbled back and leaned against the sofa, holding his head in both hands. "She's fading away. I don't know if I can make it without her. I love my baby girl. We both love our baby girl. She's grown up to be a beautiful woman and mother. I'm so proud of her. I've given her nothing to be proud of."

I would have liked to agree with him, but I knew Harlow wouldn't agree. So I spoke for my sister, who didn't have the ability to handle this herself. "You're wrong. She's proud of you. She's always been proud of you. And when she found out that you stayed by her mother's side through all this, it rocked her. She knows you love her mother. She's seen it, and that makes her even more proud of you. She saw a side of you she never knew existed. We all did."

Kiro rubbed his face and gave a frustrated roar before letting his hands fall to his side. "Did Dean call you? I don't need this shit right now, son. Why can't I deal with this the only way I know how?"

His way of dealing was getting trashed and upsetting Harlow. "Your way affects my sister, so that affects me. Dean didn't call me. Rush paid me a visit. Grant was worried about his wife. He'll protect Harlow any way he can. Surely you can understand that? Your little girl is loved just as fiercely as you love Emily."

At the sound of Emily's name, Kiro flinched as if it pained him. "What is it you want me to do? Be fucking Superman? I'm not motherfucking Superman! I've never been. Can't start now just because you come in here demanding it."

Kiro had tunnel vision. He was hurting, and that was all the man could see. He was losing Emily, and he could accept nothing more. I wanted to grab the man and shake him. Instead, I clenched my hands at my sides and took a deep breath to calm my frustration. "Do you want Harlow to lose you both? Do you think she can handle that? Do you want her brokenhearted? Don't you want to be a part of your granddaughter's life? Here's your chance to be the man Emily would have wanted you to be. You and I both know you weren't the father she would have wanted for Harlow. You can't save her, but you can grant her the one thing we both know she'd want. She would want you to be the best damn grandfather on the planet for Lila Kate."

"*I'm* the best grandfather on the planet. He'll have to be second," Dean spoke up as he kept playing on the Xbox.

Seriously? Did the man not realize this conversation was important?

"Fuck off, asshole," Kiro grumbled.

"Just setting him straight," Dean replied.

A hint of a smile touched Kiro's lips. "I want to make Emily proud. She loves Lila Kate. She brightens up whenever Harlow brings her to visit. If she could, she'd be the fucking best grandmother there ever was."

"I won't argue with you on that one. Emily was special," Dean said.

"*Is* special," Kiro snapped. "She *is* fucking special."

Dean tossed down the remote control and turned to look at Kiro. "She *is* special, Kiro. But we both know she's not the same. The Emily who left the day of the accident didn't return the same. She's been locked in that body, unable to function, for twenty-three years. You've held on to her longer than any doctor believed possible. To want to keep her here like that is selfish, man. I miss her, too. She made you a better man. That man was lost twenty-three years ago, too. The boy is right. You can't save her. But you can damn well make her proud of you. Don't you want her to be thankful that she had a life with you? Of course you do! You would do anything for that woman. Do this for her. Fucking do this. For. Her."

I didn't need to say more. Dean had said it all. Perfectly. He'd lived in a world where my father had loved a woman and been happy. He knew things I didn't. Seeing Kiro through Dean's eyes was enlightening.

"She'd want me to be strong. She'd expect it," Kiro said, staring at the floor in front of him.

Neither of us said a thing. We let him take it all in. Dean had stood up from his spot on the sofa, and we looked at each other over Kiro's bent head. We both wanted our message to get through to him.

"I want there to be a heaven. I want it for her. She should be dancing and laughing. She has the best laugh. I want there to be a place where she can have all that. Tell me that when this life ends, it's not over, that she has a new life ahead of her, full of all she was robbed of in this one."

I swallowed through the emotion constricting my throat. God, I never wanted to go through this. Kiro had been an asshole most of my life, but no one deserved to deal with pain this intense.

Dean walked over and threw his arm over Kiro's shoulder. "There's a heaven, man. There has to be a heaven for angels. And Emily was an angel. She was yours. It ain't over after this life."

Kiro closed his eyes and nodded. "You're right. My angel will be OK. She'll dance again."

Dean glanced over at me and nodded. Kiro was going to make it. He had a hard road still ahead, but he was now focused on making Emily proud of him. That was the only thing that could shake him out of this. He never wanted to let her down.

Reese

I was tucked into bed and holding my phone in my hand, waiting for Mase to call, when it finally rang and the image of his cowboy boots showed up on my screen.

"Hey," I said, sitting up, excited to hear his voice. When he got home, I was going to tell him about my picnic with Henry and Captain; it would be too hard to explain over the phone.

"Hey, baby. I'm heading home in the morning. I spent the day with Kiro. We had a breakthrough this afternoon once he finally got out of bed, but he's so volatile. I decided to stay and make sure he was good. I miss you."

"I miss you, too. I'm glad things are better with him. Was it hard?" I wished more than once today that I could be there with him.

"It wasn't easy, but I think I understand him better now. He'll never be my dad. I have one of those. But I felt something today I've never felt for the man before. Compassion."

Mase was a compassionate man. I couldn't imagine how awful his father had to have been to not get any compassion from his own son. I knew he hadn't spent much time around him growing up, but still. "Then the trip helped you, too," I said.

"Yeah, I think it did," he agreed. "But I want to be home with you."

"I want that, too."

"Are things OK there? The job still good?"

"Yes. The job is great, and I've been fine here. I ate dinner with your parents tonight."

"Good. I love you, and before you say you love me more, that's not possible."

Smiling, I tucked the covers under my chin. "I don't think so."

He chuckled. "I'll be on a plane first thing in the morning. Expect a lunch guest."

A sick knot settled in my stomach, reminding me of my other lunch guest who always popped up. I would have to tell Mase about all that when he got home. I wanted to keep my job, but I also didn't want Mase in the dark about anything.

"I'll look forward to it," I told him. "Love you."

Once we hung up, I lay in bed staring at the ceiling, wondering if Mase would react badly to Captain showing up at my office regularly with lunch. He hadn't done anything wrong, really, but would I be OK with a woman bringing Mase lunch and eating with him? No. The answer was no way. I'd be jealous.

I had to tell Mase. There was no question.

By ten in the morning, I was getting anxious. I was ready to see Mase. It had only been a few days, but every time the office door opened, my heart sped up. Then Piper would be there, and I'd smile and pretend I wasn't completely disappointed. He had said he'd be back by lunch.

Two more hours until lunch.

Just as I picked up the phone to return some calls, the door opened. Before I could get excited, Captain's face appeared, and my face fell. Not who I was hoping to see.

"Don't look so heartbroken. I'm not that ugly," he said with a smirk.

I didn't respond to that. Instead, I used my most professional tone. "What can I help you with?"

Captain cocked an eyebrow as he sat in the leather chair across from me. Not where I wanted him to sit. I wanted him to tell me what he needed and leave. Fast.

"Do you get to leave for lunch today?" he asked, leaning back and crossing his right ankle over his left knee like he was getting comfortable.

"No," was my clipped response.

He looked amused. "I thought we called a truce. We were going to be friends. You aren't acting very friendly."

I had never said I was going to be his friend. "I agreed to work with you. I didn't say I'd go out to eat with you."

"You liked the picnic yesterday," he reminded me.

"I liked Henry," I corrected him.

He nodded as if he already knew that. "I knew you would. He's a great kid."

I also got why he had brought Henry to meet me. It had been a nice thing to do. I appreciated it, but I still felt wrong about having anything other than a working relationship with him. Something about the way he looked at me made me feel he wanted more. I didn't care what he said.

"Why don't you drive?" he asked, pulling me out of my thoughts.

"Because I haven't been able to read and write until recently. Couldn't take the driver's test."

He reached into his back pocket, pulled out two thin books, and leaned over to place them on the table. One was a driver's handbook for the state of Texas. The other was a permit handbook. "You can read now. Read these."

I reached for them. I had meant to get these. The idea scared me, but now that they were here on my desk, it wasn't that terrifying. Captain had gotten them for me before I had even told him why I didn't drive. Why did he have to do such nice things for me?

"I don't expect a thank you. Just read them. You can pass the test, Reese. I know you can."

He didn't expect a thank you. I stared down at the books in front of me. I wasn't sure what to say. He was going out of his way to help me. He didn't need to be thinking about me. He didn't need to help me. But he was, and I wasn't sure how to stop that.

"Thank you," I said, because he did deserve that. "I've been meaning to pick these up."

He nodded. "Good. I'm glad you're ready to take another step in that direction."

I'd started to say something when the door opened, and I looked up to see Mase's face. My heart leaped at the sight of him, but as his gaze swung to Captain, I went from giddy to sick to my stomach.

"What the fuck are you doing here?" he asked as he stepped into the room, filling it up with his presence.

Captain dropped his propped-up foot to the floor and stood up. He was at eye level with Mase. "Came to drop

something off for Reese," Captain said, as if he wasn't bothered at all.

"Doesn't look like that," Mase snarled. He swung his gaze
to me. "He bothering you?"

This was a trick question. If I said no, then Mase would
think something that wasn't true. But as I glanced down at
the handbooks on my desk, I knew I couldn't very well throw
Captain under the bus.

"Mase, it's OK. He was dropping off some handbooks he
thought I might need. Nothing more," I explained.

I shot Captain a quick glance, and he looked surprised that
I hadn't said he was bothering me. Mase was frowning—at me
or my response, I wasn't sure.

"Does he visit you often to bring you things he thinks you
need?" Mase asked, his voice holding a warning. He wasn't
happy, and this was not the way I wanted to explain my relationship with Captain to him.

"I just bring her lunch a couple of times a week," Captain
said.

The fire that lit in Mase's eyes didn't bode well. Why had
he said that? "You do what?" he asked slowly as he turned his
glare to Captain.

"I have to bring her paperwork to file, and I sometimes
bring her food, too. Better than those damn turkey sandwiches
she eats."

Mase stood so still I was afraid of what he would do next.
"I think it's time you leave," he said in a hard, clipped tone.

Captain glanced at me. "Guess it is," he replied, and winked
at me. He freaking winked at me before walking past Mase
with a smirk on his face. I wanted to kill him.

Mase turned to me. He just stared at me silently for several moments, and I started to open my mouth to explain several times, but nothing came out.

"You didn't think that telling me another man brought you lunch was important? Or that he visits you so often?"

I had been planning to tell him. Tonight. I had planned it all out. "I wasn't . . . I was . . . I didn't . . ."

He held up his hand to stop me. "Never mind. I'm not listening to this. I just went through some emotional shit, and I don't need this right now. I need a fucking break," he said, then turned and stormed out of my office.

I stood there, watching the door slam behind him as tears spilled free and ran down my face. What had I done?

Mase

My heart was pounding in my ears as I stalked from my truck down to the stables. What the fuck had I just walked in on? Was I overreacting? I'd given Reese a chance to explain herself, and she'd stammered. She hadn't been able to explain. She had almost seemed to be defending that asshole.

Did I trust her? Yes! I never had a reason not to. She was my Reese. She was so damn sweet. How the fuck did this happen? What was wrong with that motherfucker that he thought it was OK to bring her lunch? He knew she was taken. What was the purpose behind it?

He wanted what was mine. I picked up a saddle, slung it against the wall, and shouted a string of curses. This was not what I had wanted to come home to. I should be kissing Reese and holding her close so I could smell her. But she'd been hiding something. I could see it in her eyes.

Fuck me. Was I that blind? Did I assume because I had found her lost and broken that she would never want to explore more? Had I just been a way for her to heal? Was she curious about others? I felt sick as I even thought about it. I didn't want her to be fucking curious about other men.

That stupid motherfucker wasn't ugly, either, and he knew

it. He was using his looks to rattle her, too. And she was rattled. It was working. I leaned back against the wall and inhaled a painful breath. I was her first everything. She'd never let anyone else get this close.

Was I being selfish to not let her go, if that was what she wanted? Was I caring for her like a possession and ignoring her needs? "Fuuuuuuck!" I yelled as pain sliced through my chest.

I wanted to be overreacting. Was it because I was mentally exhausted from dealing with Kiro? Everything replayed in my head.

"I just left her there," I whispered out loud, knowing she had no way to come after me and explain. I hadn't even given her a moment to get her thoughts together. She had looked as surprised as I was.

I couldn't leave her there all day to worry about this. She hadn't done anything wrong. Sure, she hadn't told me that she was having lunch brought to her by fucking River, Captain, whoever the hell he was, Kipling. But demanding an answer from her and then storming out when she couldn't verbalize one wasn't the way to handle it.

This was Reese. My Reese. There had to be a reason she hadn't said something before now. Maybe she was afraid I would react the exact way I just reacted. Or she could have been worried that I'd make her quit her job. She loved her job. She was proud of herself, and watching her blossom under Piper's obvious approval was beautiful.

I had to go back. I stalked back to the door, only to be stopped by Major, who was looking at me like I'd lost my mind.

"Move," I snarled, and started to push past him, but he grabbed my shoulders and stopped me.

"She's not there," was all he said. He sounded annoyed.

"What?" I asked him, shoving him back so he would let me go.

"She called Maryann. Your momma went to get her."

Reese. "Shit. Is she OK?" I asked, moving fast to get around Major and head up the hill toward my momma's house.

"She was crying so hard Aunt Maryann barely heard what she was saying. She ran for the door, then pointed at me and said, 'Go tell my son he better get himself ready to fix this.'"

I had to fix this. Reese was crying. My stupid temper.

"What the hell did you do?" Major asked.

"River Kipling was in her office. He brings her lunch sometimes. She never told me."

Major let out a low whistle. "He's a smooth one. But has Reese done anything wrong?"

"She never told me!" I yelled, wanting to punch something.

"Well, hell, Mase, if she thought you'd react like this, I can't say I blame her. You don't get worked up like this. Never seen you become an ass in my entire life. So what the fuck has happened to you?"

This wasn't me. I didn't lose my mind over every little thing. I was careful, and I thought things through. I made calculated decisions. I wasn't this off-the-handle insane man who had taken over.

"Stop yelling, and listen to yourself. You're acting like a nutcase over something that isn't that big of a deal. So he brought her food. Did she fuck him for it? No. I can answer that. She loves you. *You*. Snap out of this."

Snap out of this. Those words replayed in my head. Words I had just said to Kiro. When he was losing his mind over a woman.

I was acting like . . . my father. My entire life, I'd tried so hard to emulate the man who raised me. He was a solid man. A man who was careful and thoughtful but strong. Yet in one moment, I forgot all that and became the man whose blood ran through my veins.

I didn't want to be this man. But I understood him. I hadn't even lost Reese, and I was going crazy. What if I were faced with actually losing her? Could I recover from that? Would I become the man I looked like instead of the man who had taught me everything?

"I have to see her," I said, feeling helpless.

"Yeah, well, your momma will be here soon enough with her, and I wouldn't want to be you when she gets here. She's not happy with you."

I wasn't happy with me, either. I'd let Reese down, but I'd let me down, too. This man wasn't me.

My mother's truck came into view, and I took off running toward it. I wasn't waiting for Reese to get to me. I needed to see her now. Momma stopped when she saw me getting closer. I didn't even make eye contact with my mother; I kept my eyes on Reese. Her face was red and splotchy from crying, and that was all because of me.

If it was possible to truly hate yourself, I did.

Reese

Once the tears started, I couldn't stop.

After Mase left, sobs wracked my body, and I doubled over. He'd left me. I'd messed up. I couldn't lose Mase.

All I had known to do was to call Maryann. Staying at work was impossible. Telling Piper what was wrong with me was also impossible. She was gone for the day, and I would have to apologize later. Right now, I had to get to Mase.

Maryann hopped out of the truck and rushed to me. "What's wrong?" she asked, pulling me into a hug. I clung to her and cried harder.

Having any kind of motherly affection undid me. It wasn't something I knew, but I craved it. Maryann's arms around me made my tears come harder. Because I'd let her son down. She was comforting me and didn't know what I had done.

"Shhh, now, it can't be all that bad. Let's get you back home, and you can tell me what happened. I know my son, and when he knows you're this upset, he's going to be furious with himself."

No, he wouldn't. He was furious already. With me.

Maryann led me to her truck, and I got in obediently. Once

she was in the driver's seat and pulling out of the Stouts' ranch, she glanced over at me. "Can you tell me what happened?"

I could, but would she hate me, too? Probably. *I* hated me. I should have told him after the first time. I shouldn't have kept it a secret.

"I let Cap- . . . River Kipling bring me lunch several times. I didn't ask him to, he just—" I let out a small sob. "He would just show up with food, and I would eat with him. I don't even like him most of the time. He's arrogant. But I have to file paperwork that he brings me."

"And Mase is upset because River brings you food?"

"No . . . yes. He's mad because I never told him. I was afraid he'd be upset. And I kept telling River to stop. Sometimes he just came with paperwork for me to file, but a couple of times, he brought food. I should have told Mase."

Maryann didn't say anything at first. I began to think I'd made her mad at me, too. "Do you like River Kipling in any way other than as a friend?"

I shook my head. "No! I don't even like him as a friend. He assumes too much and ignores the fact that I don't want him to be in my office. I love Mase."

Maryann nodded. "I know you do, sweetheart. But it appears my son has let jealousy take control of him. It's not like him, but then, that just means you're different from any other woman who has been in his life. Give him time to cool down, and then he'll fix this."

"He was so angry with me," I whispered.

"No, he was scared of losing you. He was terrified that he wasn't enough for you. He wasn't angry at you."

He wasn't enough for me? He knew better than that. The

look in his eyes was definitely anger. But I didn't argue with his mother. She would see soon enough. He wasn't going to be happy to see me. I had to explain. Getting all tongue-tied and panicking wasn't going to save us.

"I never should have gotten a job," I said, thinking that none of this would have happened if I'd just stayed home.

Maryann made a *tsk*ing sound. "Don't start that, girl. You deserve a life. Mase doesn't have to be your world. He can be the most important part of your world, but you need to live, Reese. You need to feel accomplished and make your mark on this earth. I love my son, but I don't want you giving up your dreams for him."

I let her words sink in, but they didn't matter. "But he's in all of my dreams."

She nodded. "As he should be. But they're *your* dreams. You have control over them, not his jealousy. He knows that, too. He just needs to get his head straight."

We drove past the gate of the ranch, and I wiped my damp face as I prepared to face him. I was so used to seeing him smiling at me and wanting me. I didn't know how to deal with a Mase who didn't want to even look at me.

"There he is," Maryann said, slowing the truck. "Guess I should stop if the fool's gonna come running straight at me."

I glanced up to see Mase running toward the truck and panicked. Was he going to demand that I leave? Oh, God. What if he wouldn't let me on his property? I had to explain myself.

Maryann opened the truck door and started around the front to meet her son. I death-gripped the seat as if he was going to open the truck and yank me out.

When Mase saw his mother, he shot her a look. She said something to him and then slapped him on the back of the head, before walking toward the house and leaving me alone in her truck, just sitting there. I didn't want her to leave.

Mase took several long strides to my side of the truck and jerked the door open. I closed my eyes tightly and held on, thankful that I was wearing my seat belt. It wasn't much, but it was a form of protection.

A warm hand touched the side of my face, and my eyes snapped open to see Mase looking at me intently. His eyes weren't full of the anger I'd seen earlier. He looked . . . sorry. Worried.

"I am so sorry," he whispered. "So goddamn sorry."

Tears of relief filled my eyes, even though I didn't think I had any more tears to cry.

"I didn't . . . I don't even like him. I try to get him to leave. I'm rude to him. He just doesn't care."

Mase leaned in and kissed my mouth gently as he unbuckled my seat belt. "I don't doubt it," he said softly. "I was an ass. I let him rile me up, and I took it out on you. I was jealous, Reese. You're mine, and I can't lose you, baby."

I wrapped my arms around Mase tightly and buried my face in his neck. Inhaling deeply, I felt safe again. He was here. He wasn't mad at me. "I'm sorry. I should have told you. I was afraid you'd be angry."

His hand ran over my hair, wrapping the long strands around his fingers. "Guess I proved that theory correct," he said, sounding amused.

I nodded. "But I should have told you. He says he's not

flirting, but I don't know what he's doing. I've told him to leave me alone."

Mase took a deep breath. "I want to kill him."

Right now, *I* wanted to kill him. He had done it on purpose. "I think it would be better if I quit my job. That way, I don't ever have to see him."

Mase didn't reply at first. I stayed in his arms, thankful to have them around me. I didn't care what I had to do to keep this. "No. You love your job. I won't let my fear and that asshole take it away from you. But from now on, I'll be bringing you lunch."

Smiling, I looked up at him. "Really?"

He cupped my face with one hand. "Really. And I'll bring you Momma's food. It'll be better than any restaurant shit he brought you." A small laugh escaped me, and he grinned. "You're just so damn beautiful inside and out, Reese. I'm going to have to get used to men wanting what I have. They can't help themselves."

My cheeks heated, and I put my head on his shoulder. "I don't think that's the case. Captain is just . . . annoying."

"You call him Captain. Do you know who he is?"

"He's Blaire Finlay's brother. He was at Lila Kate's birthday. I found out his nickname then."

Mase frowned. "I never saw him."

"That's because we talked when you were inside with Harlow. Then he just disappeared. I figured he went inside."

"But he found you and talked to you," he said, sounding annoyed.

"I was with Blaire," I reminded him.

"Still, the dude is a dickhead."

Yesterday, I would have been ready to disagree. But after what he did today, I couldn't deny it. He had told Mase about our lunches for a reason, and it wasn't an innocent one.

River "Captain" Kipling had just become my enemy.

Mase

After dropping Reese off at the office and kissing her long and hard, I headed out to find River fucking Kipling. I'd given Arthur a call and asked him where I might find the guy. He'd told me he would be at the main offices for the Stout and Hawkins restaurant chain.

Stepping through the main door, I smiled at the young receptionist. I needed her help. "Morning," I said with a nod, tilting the brim of my hat back.

"Good morning," she said, a little too brightly.

"Arthur told me I could find River Kipling here this morning. You know where he might be?"

She didn't even ask for an ID. She nodded and pointed to a door. "Go through there; he's the third office on the right."

I winked and gave her a nod, then went to find the bastard.

I didn't bother knocking on his door. I just opened it and walked in, closing it behind me. River was working at his desk. When his eyes looked up to see me, I saw the gleam of challenge there. I was ending this shit.

"I actually expected you sooner," he said, leaning back in his chair, looking pleased with himself.

"Reese came first. I'd been away from her for a few days, and I needed to be with my girl," I said, putting the emphasis on *my*.

He smirked. "You here to stake your claim like a fucking caveman?"

God, I hated this douchebag. "I'm here to protect Reese. That's what I do. She was ready to give up a job she loves because of you. I won't let you ruin this for her. She's been through more shit than you could ever imagine. She doesn't need you upsetting her."

His face almost looked remorseful. "She's overcome her dyslexia. She's faced her demons, and she's thriving. She doesn't need someone to stand over her and keep the rest of the world out. Is she not allowed to have friends?"

She'd told him about her dyslexia? I was proud of her. She'd admitted it to someone else other than Piper and me. "Her dyslexia did hold her back for a very long time. But she's lived through a worse hell than that. Don't assume you know her. Because you don't. And if she wants me to protect her, I will. From anyone and anything. She didn't have that for most of her life, but she'll have it for the rest of it."

River frowned, leaning forward and putting his elbows on the desk. "You're doing her an injustice by assuming that because she had a rough home life growing up, she isn't strong enough to take care of herself. I know for a fact that made her a stronger person. I lived a life just like hers."

I really hated this son of a bitch. "What? Was life hard for you? Did you get slapped around a little? Leave home when you were finally old enough? Yeah, well, lucky fucking you. That's not the hell I'm talking about. Just stay the fuck away from her. You have papers for her to file? Then take them to her. But I'll be bringing her lunch every day."

River looked like he was weighing my words and deciding how to respond. His witty comebacks seemed to have dried up. "I was just being friendly," he finally said with a shrug. "Both of you got too worked-up over that shit. Trust is an important part of a relationship."

If I nailed him in his smug face, I'd end up in jail. I debated if that was worth it. "You being 'friendly' had her in tears yesterday. Sobbing tears. What you did yesterday wasn't friendly. It was a low blow, and then you walked off and left her to deal with it. That's not being a friend. It's being an asshole. No woman deserves that kind of disrespect."

He didn't respond. I needed to leave before he said something that I couldn't walk away from. One day, I'd get the chance to knock him on his ass. But this wasn't the place or the time.

I opened his door and walked out before he could say anything else.

It was lunchtime. I arrived at Reese's office with Momma's meat loaf, fried okra, and creamed potatoes. When I opened Reese's door, she looked up and beamed at me like I was the only person in her world. Before I could get through the door, she was out of her seat and hurrying toward me.

"Hey, baby," I said, holding the food out of the way so I could bend my head and kiss the prettiest lips in the world.

"Hey, smells good," she said.

"It is. Momma made it."

She gazed up at me through her thick eyelashes and grinned. "I was talking about you, but the food smells good, too."

"Careful, or I'll take some more of what I had this morning before I let you eat," I warned her, thinking about the shower we'd taken together before I brought her to work.

"I have a microwave," she said, backing up against the desk. I watched her as she began pulling her shirt off.

"Fuck," I replied, setting the food down on the empty chair. "You sure about this?" I hoped to God she was.

She nodded. "Piper's gone," she said, and she unsnapped her bra and let it fall off her arms. "And I'm wearing a skirt. Shame to waste it."

I took her face in my hands and claimed that sweet mouth before she could say anything else that made me lose my mind. When Reese decided to seduce me, it didn't take much. Just the fact that she wanted to was sexy as hell.

Tasting her was intoxicating.

She began to wiggle, and I broke the kiss to look down at her. She had dropped her panties and kicked them off as she pulled up her skirt. She was panting. "I missed you," she said.

I missed her, too, although we had just had hot shower sex five hours ago. I wasn't complaining. Slipping my hand between her legs, I trailed my fingers over her wet heat. She was more than ready.

I had started to go down on my knees when she grabbed my shoulders. "No. I want you in me. We need to be quick, and I want you now." She sounded breathless.

After yesterday, I wondered if this was her way of making that memory fade to the background. Whatever it was, I would do anything she asked of me.

After unzipping my pants, she leaned back, watching me, with her hands flat on the desk, putting her gorgeous tits on better display. I shoved my jeans down and then leaned over to cup both breasts in my hands. "Love these," I said reverently.

"Mmmm," she said, and her head fell back, exposing her neck.

I wasn't gonna last long with her all spread out for me like this. I reached for one of her legs, draped it over my arm, and pulled her bottom until it was on the edge of the desk. She was completely open to me now. Her eyes were full of need as she stared up at me.

Slowly, I sank into her as her tight hole gripped me perfectly. "Always so fucking good," I groaned.

"Yes," she agreed, lifting her hips so that I was buried as deep as I could go. "Ahhh!" she cried out when she was full.

"Reese," I said breathily, needing her eyes on me. "Look at me."

She did as I asked, and I began to move within her at a steady rhythm that I knew would bring us both to release faster than I preferred.

"Oh, God!" she cried as her mouth fell open.

I began to pump harder, loving the sound of her cries of pleasure. "This what you want?" I asked.

She reached to cling to my arms. "Yes," she panted.

"Tell me this is my pussy, Reese," I said, holding still inside her. I needed to hear it.

"It's yours," she said with a smile, wiggling under me.

Grinning, I shook my head. "No, baby. I want you to tell me this is my pussy." I lowered my head and kissed the tips of her breasts.

"It's your pussy, Mase," she said softly, but her eyes flared with excitement as she said it.

"That's right. It is. Mine," I said, grabbing her hips and moving with deep thrusts until she was crying my name and clawing my arms.

At the sound of my name tearing from her chest, I climaxed. Nothing would ever be as sexy as that sound.

Reese

By the time the weekend arrived, everything was back to normal. Captain hadn't been back to my office. He'd sent files over with Major twice, and I had started to breathe more easily.

Today Mase was going to check out two horses he was thinking of buying. I decided I would go grocery shopping. Maryann was going into town to run some errands and said she could drop me off at the grocery store and pick me up an hour later.

This was my first time shopping without Mase, and I was a little nervous about getting everything he wanted. I knew he'd never tell me if I forgot something, but I was focused on getting it just right. I liked the idea of taking care of him.

After spending a good ten minutes picking out the right fruits and vegetables, I moved toward the aisles. I didn't have to do too much reading here. I'd been grocery shopping for years, so I was good at identifying things by their packaging and labels.

"The little whore grew up." The low whisper sent ice through my veins. I knew that voice. It had been years since I'd last heard it, but I knew that voice. I couldn't move. I couldn't turn around.

"Not gonna say hello to your daddy?" Marco asked. He was

not my daddy. He was my mother's husband, but he wasn't my daddy. He had been my tormentor.

"If you get any closer, I am going to scream at the top of my lungs," I warned him, still not turning to look at him. I didn't want to see his face. The nightmares he starred in had just begun to fade. I hated that face.

A low, menacing laugh sent dread through me. "No, you won't. Do you want all these people to know what a little slut you are? I'll tell them all. How you seduced me. How you wanted sex from your own stepdaddy. Bet that rich little boyfriend of yours don't know what a whore you are. Or maybe he does," Marco said, and he touched my hair.

Bile rose in my throat. I was going to be sick. I tried to find my voice, but I was frozen in fear. Just like when I was a child.

"Maybe he likes stupid little sluts. With a big ass and big tits. Guess that's his thing."

I closed my eyes and cringed. No. He would not do this to me. I wouldn't let him. I was stronger now. I was grown. The little girl was gone.

"Took me a while to find you. But I've been watching you for a week now. I know where you live, where you work. Too stupid to drive a car yourself. Not surprised."

My body broke out in a cold sweat. Why was he here? Why did he want to find me?

"Your momma's dead. Not that you care. You ran off and never came back. Worthless bitch," he said, as he fisted his hand in my hair and tugged hard.

I had to get away from him. But I couldn't find my voice. This had to be a nightmare. He wasn't really here. This couldn't be real. I needed to wake up.

"Not even a tear for your momma? Stupid whores don't care about their mothers. But you loved your stepdaddy, didn't you, girl?" He pulled hard on my hair again.

"Let me go," I managed to say through the terror gripping me.

He laughed. "Took a long time to find you, girl. I ain't leaving you now. Did you tell him I had you first? That this body was mine first? That you walked around with those tight clothes on, taunting me, inviting me to touch you?"

My stomach rolled over, and I bent forward, feeling the sickness start to overtake me.

He pulled my head back with another jerk of my hair. "You're gonna walk out of here with me, and I won't tell him any of your dirty secrets," he said close to my ear. His breath smelled rank, like sour milk.

I reached up to cover my mouth, afraid I was going to throw up all over the groceries in front of me. I couldn't scream while fighting to keep the contents of my stomach from coming up. Closing my eyes tightly, I prayed that if there was a God and he cared at all, he'd save me. I hadn't been prepared for this.

Maybe there was a God, because, suddenly, I felt Marco let go of my hair. I jerked around and saw Captain with a look of fury on his face as his hand clamped around Marco's arm. Now that I could see Marco, he looked significantly older.

"You walk out of here and don't look back, and I'll let you live," Captain said in a quiet, hard voice.

Marco tried to jerk his arm free. "You want to get arrested for assault?" His voice was high-pitched.

Captain didn't look fazed. He continued looking at Marco like he was the lowest form of creature on earth. "You scream, and you won't see another sunrise. Try me, old man. Fucking. Try. Me."

I believed him. There was no smirk. No smile. The expression on his face was that of a man with no soul. He was cold, and he was making sure Marco saw that, too.

I backed away.

"You go on and get your groceries, Reese," Captain said. "I'll walk this worthless shit outside. He won't be back. I can promise you that," he said without taking his eyes off Marco.

Then he began walking with his hand still gripping Marco's arm.

I stood and watched until they walked out the front door. Then I pulled my phone out of my pocket and called Mase. I was about to shatter, and I wasn't sure I could make it to the door before I did.

Mase

I broke every speed limit imaginable by the time I got to the ranch. Momma had gone back to get her as soon as Reese called to tell me what had happened. I had kept her on the phone while texting my mother to get to the store immediately. All Reese had been able to say was that her stepfather had been there.

And that River Kipling had been there and forced him outside.

She was terrified, and I wanted to get my hands around her and hold her. If I had thought for a second that sick, pathetic excuse for a human would come to find her, I'd never let her out of my sight.

My head kept jumping to the worst-case scenario. What if River hadn't shown up? Fear consumed me. I couldn't think about that. I hated River, but I owed him one now.

My momma's truck pulled into the ranch just before I did, and I stayed right on her tail until she parked. Then I jumped out and ran for Reese. The moment I opened the door to Reese's side of the truck, she launched herself at me and began sobbing while holding me in a death grip.

My momma didn't know the details, but I knew that after seeing the reaction from Reese, she could guess easily enough. I looked at her over Reese's head. "I'm taking her to the house," I told her. She'd have to wait for an explanation.

Momma nodded and headed to her house, leaving us alone.

"I'm so sorry, baby," I said, feeling helpless as I held her against me.

She only sobbed harder. If I'd been there, I'd have killed the man. I wanted to see him dead. He'd marked her life, and he had come back to reopen old wounds. The sick bastard.

Glancing up, I saw another truck headed our way. I recognized it as River Kipling's. As much as I didn't like him, I understood his need to come by and check on Reese. He'd seen it. He had saved her. And I would have to find a way to accept him.

He stopped his truck, and Reese jumped in my arms at the sound of his door opening and slamming shut. She was spooked. I had to get her home so she'd feel safe.

"Is she going to be OK?" River asked, keeping his distance.

I would do everything in my power to make sure she was. She'd overcome this terror before. She could again. "I'll make sure of it," I replied, knowing I had to say more. He deserved it. "Thank you. For what you did."

He didn't even acknowledge my words. His eyes were on Reese's back, his jaw clenched. "I heard him. I was in the next aisle over, and I heard him. Did he . . . was he responsible for putting her through hell?"

I only nodded.

River nodded back, then turned and returned to his truck. Without a word, he drove off.

I picked Reese up in my arms and took her to my truck. She needed to be home.

I sat with my back against the headboard and Reese in my arms. Her head was against my chest, and her breathing had slowed. She was asleep and had been for more than an hour, but I hadn't moved her.

If it took weeks, hell, if it took months, we would sit here like this. I'd hold her as long as she needed. I wanted her feeling safe again. I wouldn't let fear own her. I'd love to erase it from her memory so she'd never feel like this again.

Once she was calm and rested, I was calling the police. She needed a restraining order. I was also putting more security around the ranch. I would need to talk to Piper about making sure she was never left alone at the stables. Better yet, I was teaching her to shoot. She was going to have a gun.

There was a knock on my door, and my mother's voice called out my name softly. I couldn't answer, for fear of waking Reese. Momma walked to the open door and saw me there with her. Her eyes were full of worry.

"Who was he?" she asked in a whisper.

"Her stepfather," I replied.

Mother shut her eyes tightly. "Oh, God, no," she said, and her eyes filled with tears.

"Yeah," was all I said to confirm what she was thinking.

Momma covered her mouth to muffle a sob. "Oh, Mase, did you know?"

I nodded. "She told me before we ever . . ." Momma knew what I meant without me having to say it.

"You just stay here and take care of her. I'll bring food. Dad will take care of the stables," Momma said.

"Thanks," I told her, although we both knew I hadn't planned on going anywhere. I wouldn't be leaving Reese's side.

Momma walked over and bent down to kiss Reese's head, then did the same to me. "That's a horror no girl should ever know," she whispered.

"Makes me feel helpless," I admitted. I wanted to fix all her problems. I wanted to make everything OK for her. But how did I fix her past?

Momma ran her hand over my hair. "You are what she needs. Don't feel helpless. Just be here with her."

"Done. She's got me."

Momma nodded, then turned and left the room.

The house was silent after she walked out. I continued to make a mental list of things that I needed to do when she was resting. I would make her world safe. I would do everything in my power and then some.

A small cry came from her lips, and I tightened my hold on her and put my mouth near her ear. "I'm here, and you're safe. Sleep, baby."

She calmed instantly at the sound of my voice. This was what I could do now. The rest could wait. But I'd get to it soon enough.

My world had been threatened in a second. I should have been with her. I brushed her hair out of her face and stared down at the beauty in my arms. She had faced so much pain, yet she was still just as beautiful inside. She was kind. She was honest. More important, she was mine. I'd found her. I'd found the one. The one who would change my world. Rush was right: it was all I ever wanted.

Who knew Rush Finlay could be so damn wise? He'd been the hellion rock star's son. I'd been the good one. Yet he might have said the most honest thing anyone had ever said to me in my life.

Captain

A run-down motel on the outskirts
of Fort Worth, Texas

I'd been waiting all night. I was a man of my word. Glancing at the time on the dash of the black Escalade I was driving, I saw there were minutes left before the sun rose. I had parked around the back of the building, out of sight from the front office. Not that it mattered. The attendant on duty was an older man who had drunk a bottle of tequila last night and entertained a prostitute just before coming back to his post and promptly passing out.

I'd watched every room. Only three were occupied. Two of them were closer to the office, but neither room's occupants had returned sober enough to be awake before noon. The motel sat on an empty strip of road, making things all the easier for me.

I grabbed the only thing I needed and stuck it into the holster hidden under my leather jacket.

Picking up the disposable, or what I referred to as a toss phone, I sent a single text:

The sun's up.

Then I pressed Send.

Without waiting for a response, I got out of the vehicle and headed to the room I'd been watching all night. The paint was peeling from the worn door. It was number 45, but the 4 was missing. There was only faded paint where it had once been. I stepped back and, with one swift kick, opened the door.

I didn't bother with the lights as I closed the door behind me.

"What the fuck?" a groggy voice said as the fat bastard sat up in bed.

I didn't respond. He didn't deserve a response. I wasn't here to answer his questions. He was going to answer mine. I took a seat in the chair beside the window. He'd already closed the curtains, so I didn't need to do that myself.

"I'm calling the police," he said, his voice betraying his fear.

I took the gun from my waist and shot the phone, sending plastic pieces flying in several directions.

"Motherfucker!" the man yelled, jumping up. I was thankful he was wearing underwear and I didn't have to see his saggy shit. "There's a silencer on that thing," he said. And then he recognized me. His beady eyes went wider than I thought possible as he held up both hands. "I didn't do anything else. You said if I left, I could live. I haven't left this hotel room." He started rambling.

I leaned back and watched as fear began to take control of him.

"You said—" he began again.

"I said if you walked out, I'd let you see another sunrise," I replied, then reached over and drew back one of the curtains. "There. You've seen it." I let the curtain fall back into place.

"I'll leave. I won't come back." He started rambling again.

I rested the gun on my knee and glared at the man who had done disgusting things he couldn't undo. Things that made him worthless. Unforgivable. "I know you won't come back," I said evenly as I continued to watch him.

"She's a liar. She was always a liar. Whatever that bitch told you, she's lying. She stole from her mother. She broke her mother's heart—"

"I'd stop now," I interrupted him. I ran the tip of the gun along my jeans. "The moment you raise your voice, I'll silence you. Permanently."

"What do you w-w-want?" he stuttered.

"I want justice. I want Reese to live the life she deserves. I want for every dirty, disgusting fucker like you to float in your own blood. That's all I want."

He shook his head as he backed away from me. "She lied. Whatever she said, she lied. She's a manipulator. She uses her body to make men do what she wants."

"Do you know who her real father is?" I asked him, tilting my head as I memorized the fear in his eyes.

He shook his head. "No. Man knocked her momma up and ran off. I saved them. I took care of them. I was the one who kept a roof over her head. I took care of her, and she didn't appreciate it. She expected more." He was grasping at straws. Men who knew their breaths were limited said anything they could to save their worthless lives. I'd seen it before. I'd heard it all before.

"Why did you look for Reese? She left your home when she was sixteen." This was something I simply wanted to know. If there was anyone else out there who needed to be stopped, I wanted to make sure it was handled. But from all the research I'd done, it was just this sick bastard.

"Her mother, she had papers with a trust fund for Reese. She never said who it was from. I didn't recognize the name. We tried everything to cash it in, but it was impossible. We struggled to raise that girl, and she owed us. Her poor mother passed away from exhaustion. I can't pay her medical bills—I couldn't even give her a proper burial. That money belongs to me. Reese owes me that. She owes her mother that."

So he knew about the trust fund. That explained it. "When did her mother die?" I asked.

"A month ago," he said, looking less terrified. He thought he'd made some headway with me. If he only knew.

"So the bitch is dead. That's good news," I replied, as I lifted the gun and pointed it directly at his head. Standing up, I relished the pure horror in his eyes as he backed away.

"You can't . . . I told you wh-what she did. What she owes me," he said, his voice shaking.

"Reese owes you nothing. You stole her innocence, and you turned a little girl's life into a nightmare. Not to mention you convinced her she was stupid. You marked her life in a way that can never be erased. Her past won't ever disappear. It's there inside her. She will deal with it for the rest of her life."

He shook his head. "She wanted it," he began.

And that was all I could take.

The bullet left the gun silently, and for a split second, I got to relish the look in Marco's eyes as he knew his time was up. He fell to the floor with a thud, and I put the gun back into my holster. The hole in his forehead oozed blood that covered his face and began to puddle on the floor. His eyes were wide and empty.

He was the last bastard I'd send out of this world. My job was done. It was time I moved on from this. Taking out the man who had hurt Reese was the best way to close the door on this part of my life.

When it had all started, I hadn't meant to fall in love with her. I knew her heart had been taken. But she was hard not to love.

"Enjoy hell, motherfucker," I said with finality as I dropped the small printed card that had been sent to me for this moment. Then I walked out through the busted door and headed for the Escalade.

Once I got on the road and headed to my drop-off location for the Escalade, I took out the toss phone and hit the only number I had dialed from it.

"Cap," the firm voice came over the secured line.

"Done," I replied.

A sigh of relief came over the phone. "It's over," he said. I could hear the emotion in his voice. And I understood.

"Yeah, it's over."

We ended the call, and I dropped the phone onto the seat beside me.

I would miss working for DeCarlo. He'd given me a life when I was a lost kid. I owed him a lot. For the first time, I felt like I had paid him in full. The man who had sexually and physically abused DeCarlo's daughter was now dead. Reese would live the life that her father wanted her to have. He no longer needed me trailing her to keep her safe. She was in good hands.

I had no doubt Mase Manning would give her the life of a princess.

Reese

Mase kept me in the cabin for the next two days. I was beginning to think he was more shaken up over this than I was. He kept me close, and Maryann brought us food. I let him keep me cooped up inside as much for him as for me. I knew we both needed to get back to our jobs, but I couldn't bring myself to leave the house.

More than once, Mase suggested that I call my father. He thought talking to him, my nonna, or Raul would help, but I couldn't. I was afraid I'd hear their voices and be reminded of the life I hadn't been given with them. The memories of what I'd lived with instead were too raw right now. Forgiving my father for not finding me and saving me sooner was harder after seeing Marco again.

Mase didn't press me. While we were watching a movie and I was wrapped in his arms on the sofa, he mentioned going to Rosemary Beach for a week to visit. I knew he was trying to get me away from here. I had been safe in Rosemary Beach, but the fact was, Marco could have found me there. What if Marco had found me before? What if I hadn't met Mase yet? That thought tormented me.

My nightmares were back in full force. As much as I wanted

to be strong and go back to work, I knew I couldn't. Not yet. I didn't know where Marco was, and being anywhere that put me too far away from Mase seemed impossible. I hated that I was letting him do this to me. He was walking into my fairy tale and ripping it away from me. Just like he had done with my childhood and my innocence.

Until we knew that Marco had been found and was in police custody, I was afraid to live my normal life.

It was Tuesday morning when I finally told Mase that I wanted to go to Rosemary Beach. He didn't waste any time. Our bags were packed, and a plane was sent for us within hours. Mase handled Piper, and he assured me that she was more worried about me than the job.

I loved Texas. I loved being here with Mase. But Marco had tainted it. He had taken that from me. I hated him. If only I hadn't been so terrified; if only I'd screamed. If only I had hit him or reacted in some way, he wouldn't be running free. I wouldn't be living in fear.

When we landed and deplaned, Grant Carter stepped out of a silver SUV and made his way to us.

"Thanks for coming to pick us up," Mase said as Grant took one of the bags from his hands.

"You're family, man. No thanks needed." His gaze fell on me. "Glad you're here, Reese. Harlow has been planning every second of your stay. She's very excited about having you at the house."

The sincere smile on his face didn't hide the concern in his eyes. These people actually cared about me. The evidence of that emotion caused my eyes to tear up. I'd never had a real family. The one I should have been able to rely on had let me down.

They'd allowed me to live in a world full of nightmares. I wasn't going to let that keep me from having a relationship with them, but I would never be able to truly forgive my father for that.

But this family, the one Mase came from, was loyal. They were ready to open their home and their arms to me. The people in his world just kept bringing me in and accepting me. Somehow I managed not to cry. Instead, I smiled at Grant. "Thank you. I'm looking forward to spending time with Harlow, too."

Mase's free hand settled on my lower back as he led me to the SUV. When Grant had loaded our bags and walked around to get in on the driver's side, Mase pulled me close to him and held my face in one hand. "You're my family, Reese. This makes them your family. No one in this world is more important to me than you, and because of that, my sister adores you. Accept that," he said. "That's not something to cry over."

"I didn't," I said.

His small smile tugged at the corner of his mouth. "Yes, but you fought it. I watched your face. I know every expression you have, baby."

With a soft laugh, I leaned into his hand and smiled up at him. "I love you, Mase Manning."

"And that makes me the luckiest man in the world."

We walked into the Carters' home, where finger foods and sweet treats filled the table. Harlow greeted us, with Lila Kate holding on to her leg as she peered up at everyone with a curious expression. The second Grant walked into the house, though, she let go of her mother and squealed, lifting her little arms up for her daddy.

"There's my baby girl," Grant said, dropping a bag by the door and picking up Harlow's Mini-Me.

Lila Kate patted his face with both hands, grinning brightly. "Daddy!" she announced to everyone.

"She pouts when he leaves every morning. When he gets home, it's her favorite part of the day," Harlow said, smiling at her husband and daughter.

"That's 'cause she's her daddy's girl," he said with pride as he kissed her chubby little cheek.

"Without a doubt," Harlow agreed. Then she turned her smile to us. "I got a little carried away making some afternoon snacks for y'all."

"I'm starving. That looks amazing," Mase said, stepping forward and pulling his sister in for a hug. He whispered something in her ear, and she squeezed him tighter in response. Watching them together made me wonder about Nan. Why didn't she want this closeness with them?

"Puddywun," Lila Kate told Grant as she continued to pat his face.

"I'll join in a moment. Go ahead and start without me. Lila Kate wants some pudding. It's our thing when I get home," he explained.

He walked over and kissed Harlow sweetly on the mouth and told her he loved her before taking Lila Kate back to the kitchen.

Harlow turned to watch him walk away as if she'd never seen him walk before. When she turned back to us, her cheeks were flushed. They were living the fairy tale I wanted for myself.

Mase

Harlow had taken Reese shopping with the girls today. She hadn't wanted to leave me at first, and I wasn't going to make her. But Harlow was so excited about it, and Reese began to relax some. In the end, she had assured me she was fine. I told Harlow I didn't want them leaving Rosemary Beach; I wanted to be close by if she needed me. Harlow had promised they wouldn't go far, saying she just wanted to take Reese's mind off of everything.

I was headed out to play golf with Grant and Rush at Kerrington Country Club when my phone rang. I didn't recognize the number and hated the fear that came with that. I shouldn't have let Reese go without me.

"Hello," I answered, my heart in my throat.

"Mase Manning?" It was a man's voice.

"Yes."

"This is Detective Northcutt with the Fort Worth PD. Marco Halls has been found."

Relief washed over me. They had found him. The bastard wasn't running free. "We've pressed charges, and Reese has a restraining order. What's the next step?" I was ready to end this. I wanted the man behind bars. I just wasn't sure that was going to happen.

"He's dead," Northcutt said.

Inhaling deeply, I let it sink in. The son of a bitch was dead. Holy shit.

"He was found this morning by the maid at the motel he'd been staying at. He'd been dead for a couple of days. No one knew. He'd paid for the room up front and asked for privacy; she only went in there because he was supposed to check out today."

"How?" I asked, reeling from pure relief. He'd never get near Reese again.

"Gunshot to the head. Single shot," he replied. "You were, of course, the first suspect, but we've been to your house to question your relatives. We spoke with Mrs. Colt and Mr. Colt, along with a Major Colt, who informed us that you and Reese didn't leave the house for two days and that you recently flew to Rosemary Beach, Florida, to visit your sister. We will be checking into that, but as of right now, you're no longer a suspect. It appears this man had more than one enemy. Signs show he was involved in drugs, and we believe this could have been someone he owed money. Any information you have on him would be helpful."

"Of course. But Reese hadn't seen him or her mother since she was sixteen, when they kicked her out. When she ran into him at the grocery store, that was the first time she'd seen him. It really shook her up. We don't know anything about the man except what he did to Reese when she was growing up."

"That's what we assumed. The killer didn't seem to act on

emotion. It was well planned and well covered up. This has all the markings of a professional kill. Which means we may never find out . . ." His voice trailed off. I could tell by his tone that he didn't want to know. He had Reese's statement, and he knew what that lowlife fucker had done to her.

But a professional kill? Who the hell had this man pissed off? And what if they knew about Reese? Would they think she had something of his that they wanted? Fuck. My relief turned to fear again quickly. "If this was professional, could they be after Reese next, thinking she knew something?" I had to get her and bring her to safety. Wherever she was, I needed to find her.

The detective cleared his throat. "There was something left behind that leads us to believe Reese is safe. It's also something that connects him to the drug trade. We've seen this calling card before," he said in a lowered voice.

"What? What do you mean?" I pulled the phone away from my mouth and looked at Grant. "I need to get to Reese—now."

He nodded and turned the truck around.

"There was a note. It had no prints on it, and it wasn't written by hand. It simply said *For My Little Girl*."

I let out a heavy sigh and closed my eyes as my head fell back. What the hell had happened? Whose little girl had that sick bastard messed with this time?

"Once you're back in Fort Worth, we need you both to come in and answer some questions."

"Yes, of course," I replied. "Were there prints anywhere?"

"Like I said, it was a professional job. There was no trace left behind. All we have is this note. Which . . ." He paused. "The note is a calling card explaining the reason for the death.

It's something that we've seen before. Many times. We're positive it's the same stock and ink. It's gone through testing. I just can't tell you more."

That note. The only thing I had to hold on to that told me Reese was safe. Whoever had killed Marco wouldn't have a reason to come after Reese. I doubted anyone even knew she was a part of his past.

I ended the call just as we pulled up to a small café where Harlow was waiting with Reese outside. There was concern on Reese's face, but I needed her with me. I wanted to hold her close while I thought things through.

"Hey," she said, hurrying toward me the moment I stepped out of the truck. "What's wrong?"

I pulled her to me and inhaled deeply, letting my heart rate slow down.

"What's wrong?" she repeated against my chest.

Nothing was wrong. She was here. She was safe. And someone else had made sure she was safe for good. "He's dead," I said. "Marco is dead."

She pulled back and looked up at me with shock and hope mingling in her eyes. "What?" she asked in a whisper.

"He's dead," I repeated. I decided not to give her details. Not now.

"Oh, my God," she whispered, and then let out a sob. "He's gone. He's gone forever?"

I nodded, understanding her emotion. "It's over, baby," I told her as I held her head in my hands and thanked God she was safe. And she was mine.

Reese

My head hurt, and I was ready to go home. The detective assigned to Marco's case had questioned me about everything. My mother, my real father, my father's family. I'd had to tell him exactly what Mase and I did during the two days after Marco assaulted me in the grocery store. Remembering it all was difficult, but I tried to give them as many details as possible.

I felt guilty telling them that Captain had been the one to walk Marco out. I didn't want him pulled into this. But they already had that information from eyewitnesses, and Captain had already been questioned; whatever his alibies were, they were solid.

Once we were cleared to leave, the detective gave me a fatherly pat on the back. I didn't hope they caught the person who killed Marco. I was thankful he had gotten away. I had been shown a card that said simply *For My Little Girl* and asked if I could identify the person who had left it. I had never seen a card like that in my life, although it hurt my chest to look at it. It was my fault that someone's little girl had been hurt by Marco. I had never told anyone about what happened to me before I met Mase. Marco had been free to keep terrorizing little girls because of my silence.

Mase kept me close as we walked out to his truck. "You need a long bubble bath. Then I'll give you a massage. This day is over. It's all over. You can live your life without him now."

I nodded. He was right. This was it. My life really started right now. Marco and my mother were gone, never to return. I was letting my memory of the life I had lived with them go, too.

"I want to see my dad," I told him. There were things I needed to say to him. Things I hadn't said before because I was just so happy to have a family. But for me to truly move on from my past, I had to let my father know how I felt. And that I forgave him.

"When? I'll get us a flight out as soon as possible."

"Not yet. Just soon. Let's go home and get back to our life first."

"Whatever you want, baby."

Over the next two weeks, life fell back into place. Mase brought me lunch every day, and Captain hadn't set foot in my office again. He either left paperwork for me in a file on the table outside the door, or he sent Major to bring it to me. I wasn't on edge anymore, and the emotional trauma I'd dealt with when Marco returned had begun to fade.

It was a Sunday afternoon when everything changed. Again.

Mase and I had spent a lazy morning together, and then he'd left to check on some things down at the stables. After the incident with Marco at the grocery store, we weren't just low on food, but we were also nearly out of paper towels and shampoo. While going through the bathroom to make sure there wasn't something else we needed, I saw the unopened box of tampons I'd bought last month.

Staring at them, I tried to remember when I should have started my period. I grabbed my birth-control pills out of the medicine cabinet and checked them. Two weeks ago. I should have started two weeks ago.

My hands trembled as I put the pills down and walked to the bedroom so I could sit down a minute. I'd been through a lot two weeks ago. My mind had been on everything but starting my period. I'd just missed that one pill the morning after seeing Marco.

I'd taken two the next day, though. We hadn't even had sex that night. I'd been a mess. Something had to be off. I couldn't be pregnant.

Putting my hand on my stomach, I let myself imagine for a moment that I was. That I was carrying Mase's baby. Joy coursed through me, but it was quickly replaced by unease. Mase hadn't even asked me to marry him yet. He wasn't ready for a family. I couldn't force this on him. He trusted me to take my birth control, and I'd let him down.

How could I be a mother if I'd never had one myself? I had no example of a mother. The one I'd been given hadn't been anything I would want for my child. Touching my stomach, I knew I had to go to a doctor. Without Mase. There was no reason to panic if I didn't have to, but how could I go see a doctor without telling someone?

Piper. I'd ask Piper tomorrow at work if she could take me. I trusted her, and I knew she'd understand. Well, I thought she'd understand.

I shoved the tampons back under the counter and finished

my list. I couldn't worry about this now. There was a chance I wasn't pregnant. I could just be late. I would hold on to that until I couldn't.

"Hey, baby," Mase called out as the front door opened.

I took my list and walked back into the living room. Seeing him standing there in his dusty jeans, cowboy hat, and boots never got old. Believing that he was mine was hard sometimes.

He smirked and walked over to me. "You keep looking at me like that, and we won't make it to the grocery store like you wanted to."

I knew exactly what we would do instead, and as tempting as that was, I was too scared to chance it. What if I wasn't pregnant but still could get pregnant after messing up my pills? I patted his chest and smiled up at him, hoping I didn't show the worry in my eyes. "We need groceries," I reminded him.

He lowered his head and claimed my mouth with a soul-searing kiss that made me forget everything but how good he made me feel. "Whatever you want," he whispered near my ear, then gave me a swat on my bottom. "God, I love that ass," he added.

I held up the grocery list. "Priorities," I told him, and I walked over to pick up my purse.

"I got one priority, and it sure ain't a damn grocery list," he said in an amused tone.

Was it possible to love someone as much as I loved Mase? Was it even healthy?

Mase

Reese called to tell me that Piper was taking her out for lunch on Tuesday. I was glad she was bonding with Piper. I wanted her to have friends here. This would be our world, and having Reese fit into it was important. I needed her to love it here as much as I did.

When lunchtime arrived, I headed up to Momma's to get something to eat. Aida's truck was parked outside, and I paused. If there was going to be drama, I wasn't sure I could deal with it today.

She hadn't left on good terms, and I wasn't sure why she was back. But then again, I didn't want to confront her in front of Reese later. Reese had dealt with enough this past month.

Sighing, I hoped this wasn't going to ruin my lunch. When I stepped through the door leading into the kitchen, Momma turned to give me an apologetic smile. She had been expecting me; I'd called to let her know I didn't need her packing a lunch for me and Reese today and that I'd just be eating with her.

Reluctantly, I turned my gaze to see Aida sitting at the table across from my stepdad. "Dad," I said, then, "Aida."

"You got that list ready for me to give to Johnson? He'll

be by later today." Dad knew about the drama with Aida, and talking ranch stuff was his way of keeping things level.

"Yeah, I'll get it to you after lunch," I assured him, then walked over to kiss Momma on the cheek and take the plate she had been fixing for me. "I got this. Sit down and eat."

"Sorry," Momma mouthed as she let me take the plate from her. She hadn't been expecting Aida, either. I nodded and finished filling my plate before turning to the table to sit down.

I figured ignoring Aida was pointless and tense for everyone. "So, what brings you down here, Aida?" I asked before taking a bite of the creamed potatoes.

She stiffened some, and I could see the nervous look in her eyes. We never used to be like this. It was a shame she'd messed up our friendship. "I missed everyone. Thought I'd come to see how things were," she said.

I nodded and took a bite of biscuit.

"You ready to start back at school?" Momma asked a little too cheerfully.

Aida shrugged. "Not really. I don't know what I want to do, so college seems pointless."

"Well, it's not. You need to build a solid foundation so you can be anything you want to be," my stepdad piped up.

Aida nodded. She wasn't going to argue with him. "That's what my mom says," she said with a pout.

"It's true," was Dad's response.

I focused on my pork chops. I didn't have anything to add to this conversation.

"I expected you to be engaged by now," Aida said, and I stopped chewing for a second to let her words sink in. What was she trying to imply with that comment?

Once I finished my bite, I took a long drink of sweet tea and turned to look at her. "Not yet," I replied.

A pleased smile touched her lips. Was she taking that as an in for her? Surely not. We had gone over this already.

"Let's not discuss Mase's personal life. When he's ready to get engaged, he will," Momma said with a smile that didn't meet her eyes. She was annoyed with Aida, too.

"I was just wondering if he'd decided to put a ring on it or not," Aida said with a shrug, then took a drink of her water while her gaze stayed on mine.

I didn't want to give her an explanation, but I also didn't want her thinking she had any hope. "When I think Reese is ready for that question, I assure you, I'll ask it. I'm giving her time. She's been through a lot lately," I said. The annoyance in my voice was obvious.

Dad cleared his throat, and I glanced over at him. "Thinking of starting to breed the pygmy goats. Why don't you meet me over at the east end and let's brainstorm how to do that? Besides, your momma's been keeping on at me about wanting goats."

Change of subject. Thank you, Dad. I nodded. "Sounds good. I like the idea."

"Oh, goody," Momma said, beaming at Dad.

He gave her a wink, and I watched my mother blush like a young girl with a crush. That was one of the reasons I loved this man. He loved my momma the way she deserved to be loved. Kiro had never loved her, but I was thankful for that. The life she'd been given was so much better than what she'd have had with Kiro. I had a better life than I would have had with Kiro, too.

"I have a boarder coming with two Appaloosas in thirty minutes, so I need to get back down to the stables. Mind if I take this last pork chop and a glass of tea with me?" I asked Momma as I stood up.

She jumped up, grabbed a paper towel, wrapped a biscuit in it, and handed it to me. "Take this, too."

"Yes, ma'am," I agreed. "Thanks for lunch. I enjoyed it."

She nodded, although that was what I always said when I left the table. She'd taught me that at a young age. Always thank the cook, and make sure they know you appreciate the meal they served you.

"Can I come down and see the horses?" Aida asked.

"You need to stay here and eat. Leave the boy alone, Aida," Dad said.

Relieved, I took my hat off the hook by the door and put it back on before heading outside. I'd made it through the meal, and Aida had only been slightly annoying. If she'd just leave before Reese got back home . . .

I'd missed my lunch with Reese today. I loved getting to see her and hold her in the middle of the day; it helped get me through the rest of it. Pulling my phone out of my pocket, I called her. At least I could hear her voice.

Reese

I glanced down at my phone to see the image of Mase's boots on the screen. I couldn't answer. Not yet. Not now.

Piper hadn't asked any questions when I'd walked out of the doctor's office. She'd let me sit in silence. I owed her an explanation, though. She had set up an appointment for me with her doctor and got me in fast. No questions asked. Then she had taken me during work hours.

I hit the Silent button, put the phone back on my lap, and stared out at the road.

"Sweetie, that man loves you. He worships the ground you walk on. Don't be afraid to tell him. He'll be thrilled," she said softly as she reached over and patted my leg.

Piper wasn't stupid. She had guessed why I needed to see the doctor and what the outcome was without my saying a word. I guessed it was kind of obvious. I turned to look at her. "He hasn't even asked me to marry him. All I've done is add more stress to his life. How do I tell him this?"

Piper frowned. "From where I'm sitting, Mase Colt goes out of his way to make you happy. He's so afraid of losing you he can't hold on tight enough. This isn't going to be bad news for him. Trust me."

She didn't know everything. She didn't know all the baggage that came along with me. Mase loved me, I knew that, but he wasn't ready for more. He wanted us to live together and enjoy the now. He wasn't planning the future. But here I was, with our future inside me. "I need time to adjust to this myself. I'll tell him. I'm just not ready," I explained.

Piper sighed. "It's your decision, but he's gonna want to know."

He would. I knew he would want to know. But would he be happy? Or would I just add more baggage on top of everything else? I didn't want this baby to be any less than adored. I wanted him or her to have the life I didn't get. I wanted to give my child the life that Mase was given.

"Don't wait too long. The longer you wait, the harder it will be to tell him," Piper said.

I nodded. She was right. I'd have to tell him soon. But first, I needed to know that I had somewhere to go if he wasn't ready. I didn't have just me to worry about anymore. I had another life I was responsible for.

It was time we went to visit my dad.

Mase had called again when I got back to work. I had answered the phone that time, because if I kept ignoring his calls, he'd show up at the barn. I didn't doubt that for a minute. I had told him lunch was great and I missed him. He'd seemed pleased with that, and we'd ended the call.

Sitting in his truck after work was different. There was this huge secret between us, and I felt guilty for not telling him. He had kissed me and held me against him when he'd gotten to Piper's. I always felt so safe when he held me.

The guilt was like a lead weight in my stomach. I was afraid I could lose here.

"In case she's still there when we get back to the ranch, I have to warn you that Aida's visiting. She was at Momma's during lunch today," he said, glancing over at me while he was driving.

I was not in the mood for Aida. Not the best timing. "OK. Did she say why she was visiting?" I asked, trying to sound like this news didn't upset me.

He shrugged. "I think she was bored. No real reason."

"Oh," was my only response.

It was time to visit my dad anyway. If Aida was there, it wouldn't matter. It just pushed my decision. "Can we visit my father now? I think I'm ready."

Mase's arm rested around my back, and his fingers played in my hair. "I'll book the flight tonight. You want to call him so he knows to expect us?"

I nodded.

He leaned down and pressed a kiss to the top of my head. "Whatever you want, baby. All you have to do is ask."

This time, when he called me baby, my hand went to my stomach. How was I going to tell him?

"Momma sent leftovers up to the house. We can eat and handle the travel arrangements. How soon you ready to leave?"

"Day after next. I need to tell Piper first and get some things finished up in the office."

"Sounds good. That gives me time to get things squared away, too."

When we pulled up into the driveway, Aida's truck was parked outside, and Aida was sitting on the porch steps. Avoiding her wasn't an option. I had no choice now.

Mase squeezed my shoulders. "Sorry about this."

Before I could step down out of the truck, Mase was there taking my hand. I let him help me down and pull me close to him as we walked toward the house. Aida stood up as we approached. Her eyes looked red from crying, and her bottom lip trembled.

"I wanted to apologize to both of you," she said, then sniffled. "I didn't mean to cause so much trouble. I came back to tell you I was sorry." She looked directly at Mase. "I miss you. I miss our friendship. I want my cousin back."

Mase's body seemed to relax beside me. "I never left, Aida. But you changed things. You couldn't accept Reese, and she's a part of me."

Aida nodded and let a single tear roll down her perfect face. "I know. I was jealous. I'd never had to share you before. I'm sorry." She glanced at me. "I really am sorry. I didn't mean to break down like I did."

"If you can accept Reese and understand that she's my life now, then we can go back to being friends. You've been my little cousin for most of my life. I care about you. I want you to be happy. I just won't allow you to hurt Reese. Ever."

Aida looked as if she were pouting. But then, she had such full lips sometimes it was hard to tell. "I won't. I promise. I want you to be happy, too."

"Then let's forget the past and start over," Mase said.

Aida beamed up at him. "Really?"

He nodded. "Really."

I wanted to believe her. But something in my gut was telling me this wasn't sincere.

Mase

Something was bothering Reese. I couldn't figure out what, and if I tried to talk to her about it, she went silent. It was almost a relief to arrive in Chicago. My hope was that she needed to see her new family, that she was anxious to see them again though nervous about talking to Benedetto about her past. I just needed to know that was what was making her act so jumpy.

I was used to her telling me things and opening up to me. This was different. It was like she'd put up a wall and refused to let me in. It scared the hell out of me. If this was because Aida was staying with my parents for a couple of weeks, then I'd send Aida home. I just needed Reese to tell me what was wrong. I felt so damn helpless.

Benedetto met us at baggage claim, and surprisingly, Reese headed straight into his arms for a hug. I had expected her to be standoffish until she had a chance to speak to him about everything that was bothering her.

"I missed you," he said with a look of joy in his eyes as he held her.

"I missed you, too," she replied as she pulled back. "Thanks for having us on such short notice.

Benedetto frowned. "Never apologize for coming to see me. My house is yours. Always, *passerotta*."

Reese's grandmother also referred to her as *passerotta*, which she had informed me was a term of endearment that meant "little sparrow."

"Nonna is very anxious for me to get you home," he added, picking up her suitcase and looking over at me. "It is good to see you again, Mase."

"Likewise, sir," I replied. I picked up my suitcase and placed my hand on Reese's back.

"I'm glad you're here. Last time, when you left, Reese's thoughts went with you. She had a hard time."

"I had a hard time leaving her here," I replied.

Benedetto seemed pleased with that answer and turned to lead us out to the waiting silver Escalade that his personal driver had pulled up to the curb.

"You both sit together in the back. I'll sit up here with Hernaldo," Benedetto instructed. "Raul wanted to come pick you up, but his afternoon classes kept him from it. He's very anxious to see you both again."

Reese strongly resembled her brother Raul. It was strange looking into his eyes and seeing some of Reese there. Her brother hadn't been bitter that he was no longer an only child but had embraced having an older sister and seemed genuinely happy to spend time with Reese.

"I look forward to seeing him," Reese said, and I knew she meant it. No matter what pain she still harbored for her father, she adored her brother.

"Nonna will want all of your attention first, of course. She's already ordered high tea for your arrival. I expect she'll be in her Sunday best," he told Reese with a wink.

Reese laughed and looked up at me. I wished she'd grown up with this life, with this loving, warm, safe family supporting her. But at least she had it now. That was something to be thankful for.

"I spoke with Nonna last week," Reese told him. "She was asking when I'd be back for a visit."

Benedetto nodded. "Oh, yes, she's been on pins and needles since your call the other day letting us know you were coming."

Once we were all settled into the SUV, the small talk continued. Reese sat close to me, letting me hold her hand in mine. Maybe this was all that had been bothering her. I hoped it was over now and I'd be able to get past that wall she'd put up.

It wasn't long before we pulled up to the iron gates of the DeCarlo estate. The first time I'd visited, I'd had to fight off feeling furious that Reese had been struggling to survive while the man who had given her life lived in total luxury. However, the pure joy on the man's face as he got to know Reese slowly dissolved my bitterness. I believed that he hadn't known where to find her. Whatever had kept him away was no longer important. He was in her life now.

Nonna opened the front door wide, and she was beaming as she called Reese's name.

"I'll help your dad. You go visit your nonna," I told her, then pressed a kiss to her lips before she turned and hurried up toward her grandmother.

"She's good for Nonna," Benedetto said behind me.

"Nonna is good for Reese, too," I told him.

He nodded, and a look of concern crossed his face. "I wish

she'd always had this family. I wish a lot of things, but I did what I thought was best."

He'd been wrong. What he'd thought was best had been a nightmare. "Reese's past is hers to share with you. But I'll tell you, anything would have been better than the life she survived."

Benedetto tensed, and pain slashed across his face. Did he know more than he was letting on? How could he know? "I've made many mistakes in this life," he said, watching as Nonna took Reese into the house before turning back to me. "But that mistake is one I can never forgive myself for. I'll go to my grave with that part of my soul destroyed."

He knew. He had to know.

"Let's go inside. Hernaldo will make sure the luggage gets to the correct rooms." Benedetto gestured for me to walk with him.

We walked in silence, and I replayed his words over and over in my head. How could he know what Reese had suffered? Who would have told him? She'd come here to tell him and unburden herself of things left unsaid. If he knew already, why didn't he let her know?

"Knowing my daughter is with a man who can and will protect her with his life is comforting to me. She loves you, and I can see that you love her. But I want you to understand that if there is ever a time when you stop loving her or you can't protect her anymore, you must bring her to me. Do you understand?"

I was never leaving or giving up Reese. Not for any reason. "I understand. But that day will never come. Reese is my life. She's my future."

Benedetto nodded. "Good. That's what I want to hear."

Reese

Nonna had kept me with her all afternoon, until Raul had returned home and insisted it was his turn to hang out with me. I enjoyed my time with them, and it pushed the conversation I needed to have with my father to the back of my mind. Benedetto was still a stranger to me in so many ways. He felt powerful yet loving. I knew he was glad to have found me, but I didn't know him the way I felt I was getting to know Nonna and Raul.

Telling him about the baby scared me. He seemed to be a very traditional man. Even though I knew he'd had sex with my mother as a fling and left me behind, he expected more from his family. How would he feel about me being pregnant and not even engaged? Would that disappoint him?

I had planned to come see him to tell him how the past had marked me. How it was hard to forgive him for leaving me with my mother. But now that didn't seem as important. I had a baby to think of. A child I would never allow to experience the horror I had lived through. I wanted this baby protected and loved. If Mase wasn't ready for this, I had to know that someone wanted us. That someone would take care of us.

Once dinner was over, I turned to my father. "I'd like to

speak with you," I said softly while the others still talked among themselves. Raul was telling Mase about a game of basketball he'd played last week.

Benedetto gave me a warm smile. "Of course. Let's go to my library."

He began to stand, and I glanced around as I did, too. Everyone was going to know we were leaving to speak alone. I didn't mean to draw attention to the matter. Especially around Mase, who would think I was going to talk to my father about something entirely different.

"I'm stealing my daughter away so I can have some time with her. This bunch demands all her attention, but I'd like some, too. Please, enjoy a cocktail in the drawing room while we have a private moment," Benedetto said, holding out his arm for me to take.

"You stingy old goat," Nonna complained, but I could see the pleased look in her eyes.

I looked down at Mase and gave him a reassuring smile. I didn't want him following us. This had to be done alone.

"If he bores you too much, remember, you can always escape by saying you aren't feeling well. Works like a charm," Raul called out as we left the table and headed down the hallway to the library.

"The boy thinks I believe him when he uses that excuse, too. I just know if he says he isn't feeling well, he's already checked out on me and isn't listening to a word I'm saying. What's the use in keeping him?"

I laughed. Hearing the two of them carry on with each other like this gave me hope that I could be a good parent. That I had it in my blood to be the mother my baby deserved.

230 F ABBI GLINES

That one day, twenty years from now, we would be joking with each other and cherishing shared memories.

Benedetto opened the library door, and I walked inside. The smell of leather and books engulfed me, and I wanted to inhale deeply. Once books had terrified me. I hadn't wanted to be near them for fear I'd be asked to read. Now I wanted to open every book and discover the treasures inside.

"Have a seat, and I'll fix us a drink. Would you like a martini?"

I shook my head. "A club soda will do."

Benedetto studied me. Instead of walking over to the bar behind two large oak doors, he stood across from me. "No drink?" he asked, watching me.

"No," I replied.

He let out a sigh, and then a smile tugged at the corner of his mouth. "*Passerotta*, you are to make me a grandfather." He didn't seem disappointed. He seemed . . . hopeful.

I nodded, waiting for more of a reaction.

He clapped his hands and let out a shout of laughter. "This is news to celebrate. Why did you not tell us as soon as you arrived? We could have had a celebration dessert prepared. Nonna will be tickled pink."

"Mase doesn't know yet," I said, causing Benedetto's smile to fade.

"He doesn't know? But why haven't you told him?"

Because . . . what if he left me? What if he wasn't ready? "It wasn't planned. He hasn't even proposed. He's not ready for this," I said, my fears tumbling from my heart and out of my mouth.

"That man loves you, Reese. He adores you. He would take

on an army for you. Why would you think he won't rejoice over the news that you're carrying his child?"

I sank onto the leather sofa behind me. "He says I am his future, but he never discusses it, really. A child isn't in his plans. I'm going to tell him, but if he isn't ready, I . . . I won't be able to stay with him."

Benedetto walked over and sat down across from me. "If he isn't ready, you will come to me. Nonna, Raul, and I would make sure you and your baby want for nothing. But that won't be the case. You will make that man the happiest on the planet when you tell him. He wants you forever, *passerotta*. This will be his insurance that he has you. He fears losing you even more than you fear losing him. I can see it in his eyes."

I wanted him to be right. I wanted Mase and me to share the joy and excitement of the life we had created. If only I knew he'd feel the same way.

"Tell me you will tell him soon. Trust me. Trust him. Give him this chance to prove he loves you and that he wants this."

"What if he feels pressured into doing something he doesn't want to do? Like asking me to marry him? If he'd wanted to do that, he would have by now, wouldn't he? He was raised by a mother who taught him right from wrong; I don't want him proposing to me because he thinks it's the right thing to do."

Benedetto nodded his head. "That is understandable. Men sometimes have the worst timing in the world when it comes to proposals. However, you don't have to accept his proposal if you don't think he means it. Let him wait. When you're sure he loves you and wants you as his wife for no reason other than he can't live without you, then you can say yes. But not until then."

I could do that. Just because he felt he had to propose didn't mean I had to feel that I had to say yes. We didn't have to be married, anyway. There wasn't a rule book that said we had to be married to be parents.

"OK. I'll tell him. And if he proposes, I'll say no. For now."

Benedetto smiled and patted my hand. "Watching you drive this boy crazy will be an endless source of entertainment for me. I hate that I will miss so much when you're back in Texas."

"Thank you," I said.

His expression turned serious, and I saw something in his eyes that made my heart ache. He seemed to be in pain. "I haven't been the father you deserved. I failed you. I'll never forgive myself for failing you. But know that I will use the rest of my time on earth to make sure I never fail you again. I can't change your past, *passerotta*. If I could, I would take it all away. But I can't. I can only do what is in my power. And I will use every ounce of that power to ensure that your life is full of sunlight and joy from here on out."

Tears welled in my eyes, and I tried not to blink so they wouldn't roll down my face. I didn't have to tell him about my past. Looking into his eyes, I felt he already knew. I wasn't sure what he knew, but he knew something. And it was enough.

Mase

It was late when Reese finally made it to the bedroom. I had struggled with the desire to check on her several times, but she had been with her father, and they needed that time together. This was her chance to heal from the anger and pain she carried toward him.

I was sitting on the end of the bed when the door opened and she walked in. Seeing the smile on her face helped ease my mind, and I jumped up and rushed over to her to make sure she was OK. "Hey," I said, wrapping her in my arms and inhaling her sweet scent.

"Hey," she replied. "Sorry I'm so late. We ended up talking a lot longer than I expected."

"About the past?" I asked, pulling back to look at her.

"Yes and no. We also talked about happy things. His childhood and how he met my mother. Things like that. Things I never knew or understood."

"Did it help?" I wanted it to help. It would never erase her past, but I wanted her to be able to close the door on it.

"Yes. It helped a lot." She paused, and I waited. "But that wasn't why I wanted to talk to him. I came here for another reason."

The touch of uncertainty and fear in her voice didn't sit well with me. The walls she had built were about to come down, and I was scared to find out why she had built them to begin with. What did she need to talk to her father about that she couldn't entrust to me?

"Mase, I . . . see, um, I . . ." She stopped and let out a frustrated sigh as she struggled to put words together. I watched her close her eyes tightly and inhale deeply. This wasn't easy for her, and that terrified me. What could she possibly need to tell me that was this hard?

"Reese? Baby, whatever you have to say, I can take. I'm here. Just tell me."

She nodded and opened her eyes to look at me again. "OK. I want you to know that this wasn't planned, and this is not a trap. I'd never do that. I do not expect a thing. I just . . . I just need you to believe me when I say that. I don't want you to ever think this was on purpose."

She was rambling, and I was getting more nervous by the second.

"I'm pregnant," she blurted out, and her eyes went wide, as if she couldn't believe she'd said it out loud.

That was what she was so scared to tell me? She was going to have my baby? I stared at her in awe and let my gaze fall to her flat stomach. We had created a life, and it was inside her. She was carrying it. Our baby.

"I swear, I don't expect a thing. If you aren't ready for this, Benedetto said I can stay here with him. So don't think you have to—"

"Wait, what?" I snapped my gaze back up to meet hers. "Stay with him? Why would you stay with him? We have a home. Our home. Our baby's home. You'll stay with me. Both of you."

Her shoulders slumped with a sigh, and I wanted it to be one of relief. Why she thought she had to prepare for me to kick her out I had no idea. Didn't she understand that when I said she was my future, I fucking *meant* she was my future?

"There's no pressure. It happened, and it's my fault. I forgot to take a pill that day that . . . Marco came. I took two the next day when I realized it, but apparently, that didn't work. I don't want you to think you have to do anything you're not ready for."

This woman was having my baby, and I worshipped the ground she walked on. How in God's name did she think I'd feel pressured to do anything when it came to her? I loved doing things for her. "Reese, baby, I love you. I don't say those words easily. When I tell you that I love you and you're my world, I mean it. They aren't words that I just throw around. You've given me your heart, and I thought you'd given me your trust, too. Apparently, I don't have all of you yet, and that's my fault. I failed somehow. I haven't made sure you know just how important you are to me. You're having my baby, Reese. The woman I love is carrying my baby inside of her. Do you know how fucking thrilled I am right now? You are mine." I walked over and put my hand on her stomach. "*This* is mine. And I'm not ever letting go of either of you."

Reese laid her head on my chest and let out a small sob. I cradled her against me. She was so scared of people turning on her, but she expected it. From everyone. Except Benedetto. She'd trusted him. She had told him. How did he get the trust that I didn't have? What did he do right that I had done wrong?

When I picked up the ring I had found last week and was having resized, I would prove to her that she had me. Hell, she'd had me the morning she sang off key and shook her ass in my face. I hadn't realized it then, but she'd had me.

"I'm sorry I didn't tell you right away. It was just a surprise to me, and I wasn't sure how you would react. I didn't want to force anything on you."

I cupped her face in my hands. "In this life, you will always be my number one priority. Your happiness is my goal. Never doubt me again. Promise me that," I said, needing to know that next time, she'd come to me. Not her father.

She nodded. "OK. I promise."

I kissed her lips gently. I wanted to get her naked and in-spect every inch of her body to see if it had changed. Were her hips wider and I hadn't noticed? Did her stomach show any signs? Were her breasts tender?

"I need you to do something for me," I told her, reluctantly letting go of her mouth.

"What?" she asked breathlessly.

"Get naked. Let me explore and see if I can find any changes," I said with a grin I couldn't wipe off my face.

She blushed. "Are you serious?"

I nodded. "Very."

I could see the arousal in her eyes as she watched me. She liked the idea of me touching her everywhere. Paying extra at-tention to areas she loved me to kiss.

"I'll give those sensitive nipples special attention," I prom-ised as I slid my hands to the waistline of her skirt.

"Oh?" she asked, leaning into me.

"Mm-hmm. Any other tender place that needs my expertise?" I asked, cupping her ass in my hands.

"Ahhh . . . yes." She arched into me.

"Then let's get you undressed and find out just where I need to kiss. This could take hours."

Reese lifted her hands into the air and gazed up at me. All that trust in her eyes made me want to beat my chest and roar. This was my woman. I'd never let her down.

Reese

When we left Chicago, Nonna was already knitting a baby blanket. My father had been right. She was ecstatic. Raul had also been thrilled. He kept referring to himself as Uncle Raul for the rest of our stay. But after three days, I knew we needed to get home and tell Mase's parents.

Mase had become overprotective. I kept assuring him that I could walk around and I didn't have to rest yet—I wasn't even showing. I really hoped I wouldn't get morning sickness, because I wasn't sure he could handle it.

He was also anxious to get me back to the doctor so he could go, too. He had a million questions I didn't have the answers to. The one thing he never mentioned was marriage. I was torn about that. I hadn't wanted him to propose because he thought he had to, but then his not even mentioning it worried me, too. I convinced myself that it was my pregnancy hormones and I had nothing to worry about. Even if he never asked me to marry him, he wanted me. He wanted both of us. I didn't have to wear his ring or have his last name to be his.

Getting home and telling his parents was our first priority. Maryann brought over a chocolate cream pie, and I made a pot of coffee. I could see the unease in his stepfather's eyes and the excitement in his mother's. I wanted him to just blurt it out and get it over with. I wanted them to be happy, but I worried they'd feel I was trapping Mase. That was my biggest concern.

"Thanks for coming and bringing the pie. It's been a long day of traveling, and Reese needed to rest," Mase said. I shot him a frustrated frown. He made me sound like a wimp. The reason they were here was that he insisted I get comfortable and relax.

"We never get invited over. This is a treat," Maryann said, smiling at me brightly. She was so excited about being here that I felt guilty for not inviting her over more often. I needed to make it a point to have them over more.

"I'm ready for some pie," Charlie piped up. "Let's talk and eat. She wouldn't let me touch it before we got here."

Maryann rolled her eyes and slapped her husband's shoulder. "You're being rude. They have to tell us something."

Charlie shrugged. "Well, they aren't gettin' to the point. When y'all getting married? There. Now, let's have some pie."

I froze. I couldn't breathe, and I felt sick to my stomach. I hadn't expected them to think we had news. Telling Mase had been too easy. They weren't going to be happy about me being pregnant if we weren't married.

Mase slipped his arm around my waist and squeezed me. He was watching my reaction. He could read me well. This was his way of reassuring me, but it wasn't working. I wasn't reassured. I was terrified.

"We're going to have a baby," Mase said, with pride in his voice. I wanted to crawl under the table and hide. Charlie stared at me, and Maryann clapped her hands and squealed.

"I knew it! I knew it!" she said excitedly. I moved my gaze from Charlie to Maryann and saw pure joy in her expression. Air eased into my burning lungs. At least his mother was happy.

"Doing this a little backward, aren't you, son?" Charlie finally spoke up. Those were the words I'd feared.

Mase's grip on my waist tightened. "I was unaware that I had to do this in some order. I'm an adult. This is my life."

"Charlie, this is wonderful news. We knew they'd get married. So what if the baby came before the proposal?"

Oh, God. I was going to throw up. He'd never mentioned a proposal. She was assuming something that wasn't in the works.

"He moved her in here without proposing. He's had plenty of time. Haven't you, Mase? It's a shame this poor girl has to be treated like this. Thought I raised you better."

My knees felt weak. If Mase hadn't been holding me up, I wasn't sure I'd still be standing. His stepdad was saying everything that had been haunting me and confronting Mase with it. Would this send him running? Change his mind?

"I moved her in with me because I couldn't live without her. My intentions have always been to spend the rest of my life with her. I was just taking this one step at a time."

"And you got those steps all screwed up," Charlie said. "Your momma can be excited, but I'm thinking of the big picture here. That girl deserves to have a ring on her finger if she's having a baby. She needs that security. You had a single mother for the first few years of your life. You know better than anyone how important it is to be the man your kid deserves. Fix this." His words sounded like a demand.

Mase was tense beside me, and Maryann looked shocked at Charlie's outburst. I couldn't say anything. I could hardly breathe.

"I don't want that pie. I'm going home," Charlie said, and he headed out the door.

"I am so sorry. He's just . . . he has ideas of how things should be done. He doesn't mean anything by it. He's excited about this baby. Just give him time," Maryann said.

"He's got a funny way of showing it," Mase said tightly.

Maryann walked over and hugged him, then turned to me and kissed my cheek and hugged me. "I couldn't have asked for a better mother for my grandchild. Thank you," she whispered in my ear.

As she stepped back, I wanted to burst into tears. Having her accept this and be happy about it helped. "I'm leaving the pie with the two of you. I have a man to straighten out," she said, then gave Mase an apologetic smile.

Mase didn't reply. His mother finally turned and left the house.

I had no idea what to say to him.

"He's wrong. He's got old-fashioned ways. Ignore him," Mase said, still holding on to me.

As much as I didn't want to talk, I knew I had to say something. I had to clarify that I wasn't expecting a ring. I certainly didn't want one under these circumstances. "I don't want a ring. This baby is not meant to force you into something you weren't planning on doing. I'd never allow you to be pressured to marry me. So, please understand, I won't marry you if you ask me now, not if it's because I'm pregnant. The baby can have your last name. We don't have to be married for that to happen. Just don't . . . don't think about anything he said."

Mase frowned. "I'd never ask you to marry me because I felt pressured to do it," he said, his voice sounding sincere.

Letting out a sigh of relief, I nodded. "Good."

Mase

The teardrop-shaped pale pink morganite stone was set within a halo of diamonds embedded in a rose-gold band. It was unique, and it was beautiful. It had stood out to me from the thousands of diamond rings I'd been shown, and the simple setting had struck me as perfect. I could see it on Reese's hand. I didn't need to see another ring.

Having it sized had been tricky, because the diamonds ran along the band of the ring, so it had taken a few weeks for it to be done correctly. Holding the finished product in my hand was exciting and terrifying. Timing was important, and I was afraid I'd royally screw this up.

Reese was adamant that I not propose to her because she was pregnant. If only I'd been able to give her this ring just a week ago. But I hadn't been, and all I had now was proof that it had been purchased three weeks ago. This had to be handled delicately. I didn't want her memory of our engagement to be tainted by my begging and pleading for her to believe me. I wanted it to be special. Something she would love to remember.

My mother knew about the ring—I'd told her when I found it—so she had been aware that I was going to propose before the pregnancy news came. Charlie knew that, too, now. My mother had made sure he understood how out of line he'd been. Given that he had apologized to me this morning at the stables, Momma must have been hard on him.

I tucked the small black velvet box into my jeans pocket and headed to the house. I had to plan this, and I had only three hours left before I went to pick up Reese from work. Momma was going to help me, and even Charlie was going to play a part. I just had to pull it all together.

Reese

The door to my office opened after a brief knock, and I looked up to see Aida walk into the room. I hadn't seen her since we had returned home. Apparently, my luck had run out; she'd come to find me.

"Hello, Aida," I said as she took a seat across from the desk.

"I thought we could talk privately. I have a few things I'd like to say to you. Things you need to hear, because from what I can tell, you're not that smart," she began.

Her insult stung, as if I'd been slapped. I'd heard those words a lot in my life.

"I heard you were pregnant, but I see you're still not wearing a ring on your finger. Mase isn't proposing. That should tell you something. If he was as in love with you as he claims, you'd be engaged." She smiled at me with steel in her eyes. "When a man wants you, he puts a claim on you, one the world can see. You don't have that, do you? Nope. Think about that, Reese. Think about all the sweet things he says and how he doesn't follow through. Hooking him with a baby isn't going to work. Bad idea." She stood up and tossed her hair over her left shoulder.

I had nothing to say. I didn't want to believe a word she

said, but it was hard not to. Charlie had basically said the same thing. Was this my stupidity?

"When he gets bored and moves on, I'll be waiting for him. I've been waiting for him since I was a little girl. You're not taking him away from me. He's just sidetracked. I'll get him in the end. Enjoy him while you've got his attention."

I watched as she shot me a triumphant smile and left my office with a slam of the door.

I sat staring at the closed door. Mase loved me. I knew he did. So why did her words sting? Why did I let her get to me like this? She was angry that I had Mase. That was all this was. I would not get upset and worry about it. I wouldn't.

But I did for the rest of the day.

When I walked out to see if Mase had arrived to pick me up, I was surprised to find Charlie sitting in his truck instead. He'd never sent his stepdad to pick me up before. After last night, I was nervous about getting into the truck with him. I was surprised Mase had sent him, of all people.

Gripping my purse tightly, I walked to the passenger side and climbed inside. "Thanks for coming to pick me up," I said, feeling awkward.

Charlie nodded. "My pleasure. Besides, we need a minute to talk. I was out of line last night."

He sure was. I didn't reply, though.

He backed up the truck to head out to the main road. My grip on my purse turned my knuckles white as I stared at the beige dashboard in front of me. "Seems I was speaking without knowing all the specifics. I judged Mase when he didn't deserve that. He's a good boy. He's always been so dependable, and I felt like he was letting you down. I didn't want to see him make a mistake and screw up his life. Wasn't my place to say so, though, and I've apologized to him, and he's explained some things to me. I was wrong. I hope you can forgive me."

I nodded my head. "Yes, of course," I said. I hadn't been mad at him anyway. Just embarrassed. I was glad he'd apologized to Mase, though.

"Good, good. Glad to hear it," he said, and he slowed down to drive through the gates of the Colt ranch. "Maryann ain't real happy with me right now. I've got some making up to do where she's concerned. But knowing the two of you forgive me, I think I have a chance to make my woman happy again."

Maryann loved Charlie. I had no doubt she would forgive him easily enough. I knew how easy it was to forgive a man you loved. Especially if he was truly sorry.

"Oh, one more thing," Charlie said as he pulled up in front of his house. "Mase left this for you. I think he needs you to get something out of the stables. I'll just let you out here."

I took the white envelope he was holding out for me. "Uh, all right. Thanks," I said, wondering what in the world this was about. I didn't know where anything was in the stables, and the sun was already setting. Walking up to the house in the dark across this huge ranch wasn't my favorite idea.

Charlie nodded and opened his door, then got out. I did the same as I opened the envelope to find a copy of a receipt. There was a red circle drawn around a date. It was exactly three weeks ago. The item and the price were both blacked out, but the store was Tiffany.

I had started walking toward the stables when I saw flickering candles to the left. Stopping, I turned to see that the path that led up to our cabin was lit by candles in jars. There were hundreds of them flickering in the setting sun. It was beautiful. What was going on? I started to put the receipt back but noticed another piece of paper. There was a note in Mase's handwriting: *Follow the candles.*

Confused, I turned and headed up the path toward the flickering lights. As I came to the first one, I saw rose petals sprinkled along the ground. Smiling, I bent down to pick one up. What was he up to?

I continued walking and saw red, white, and pink rose petals decorating the pathway. As the house came into view, I noticed a flat box sitting at the end of the path. It was wrapped in silver paper with a large iridescent pink bow on top. My name was written in bold print on the front of the attached card.

I carefully unwrapped it. Inside, I found the first book I'd ever read to Mase. It was a children's book that I had been given by my tutor. I had struggled the first few times I'd read it, but I had gotten better as the week progressed. Mase had cheered me on and made me feel I could do anything. It was the first time in my life I had believed in myself.

Holding the book in my hand like the cherished memory it was, I continued up the walkway and toward the steps, where the candles continued to light my path. Once I got to the door, I saw another small package wrapped identically to the first one. It also had my name on it. Placing my book down on the chair beside me, I carefully opened the package. In it was a piece of broken mirror. As I stared down at it, the day I'd met Mase came back to me, when I'd fallen and broken Nan's expensive mirror and sliced my hand open while cleaning her house. He'd been staying at her house and had taken care of me that day better than anyone had done in my entire life.

I reached up and opened the door, still holding the small box with the piece of mirror in it. Then my eyes met Mase's. He was standing just inside our living room, which was also filled with candles. He wasn't dusty and in his work clothes; he was all clean and dressed in a pair of his good jeans with a button-down flannel shirt.

"I kept it," he said.

Frowning, I tried to figure out what he was talking about.

"The mirror. I kept a piece. I didn't know why at the time. But when I cleaned it up, I kept a piece. I wanted to remember you. I didn't expect to see you again. So I kept that piece of mirror."

Wow. Oh, wow. I held the box tighter in my hands as I stared up at him.

"I kept the book, too," he said. "When you conquered it, I called your tutor and had him sell me the book. I wanted to remember you reading those words to me. How you were so shy at first but with each sentence and each day, you grew stronger and more sure of yourself. It was the most beautiful thing I've ever witnessed."

My heart felt like it was going to explode from my chest. I even placed a hand over it to keep it from breaking free.

Mase walked toward me and held out a piece of paper. It looked like a receipt. "This isn't something that a man normally shows a woman, but I need you to see that date and understand what it means. Because of timing and circumstances, it took three weeks to get from that moment to this one."

I took the receipt from his hand, but before I could look down at it, Mase was lowering himself to his knee.

No. This wasn't happening. I didn't want this. I had told him I didn't want this. I started shaking my head as tears stung my eyes. I didn't want all this sweetness to become part of a bad memory.

"I need you to look at that receipt, baby. Please," Mase said as he stared up at me.

My stomach was in knots. My throat burned, and my eyes were blurry. Had he not listened to me? I didn't want to force him to do anything. I blinked and tried to focus on the receipt. Once again, the date was circled in red. Just like the one he'd given me a copy of. It was the same receipt. However, the item wasn't blacked out on this one, only the price.

Pear-cut pink morganite ring with rose-gold band.

I reread the words and even said them under my breath as I let the information sink in. It was a ring he had bought three weeks ago.

"It was perfect for you. It just wasn't your size," he whispered.

I lifted my gaze to meet his and saw that he was now holding a ring in his right hand.

"I had to get it sized to fit your finger," he said softly.

"Oh," was all I could manage to choke out past the lump in my throat.

"Reese Ellis, you came into my life and lit it up. Everything that was dull became shiny. You changed me. You made my life complete. So please, give me all I want in this life and say you'll be my wife."

My cheeks were wet by the time he finished talking. All I

knew was that this was right. This was it. This was the way it was supposed to be. And I'd never love another man the way I loved this one. "Yes," I managed to say past the sobs that broke free.

Mase slid the ring onto my finger and stood up to claim my mouth with his.

This was the best fairy tale of them all.

Epilogue

Mase

Reese hadn't been insistent that we get married before the baby was born, but I wanted her last name to be Colt Manning before we brought a child into this world. We would be a family. The kind she and I hadn't started out in life with.

Today Harlow had come to Dallas to shop for a wedding gown with my mother and Reese. Tomorrow Reese, Harlow, and I were going to L.A. to tell Kiro about the wedding and the baby. He wasn't drinking himself to death, but Emily was getting worse, and Harlow was worried about him. I didn't want her to visit him without me, and I needed to tell him about Reese and me. It just wasn't something I planned on doing over the phone.

I wasn't sure he'd even care about the baby or the wedding, but he was my father. He should at least be told. I did the best I could with him for Harlow's sake.

Dad pulled up in front of the stables and held out my mail, like he did most days when he drove out to check our mailboxes. "Got a few things today," he called out.

I headed up the hill to his truck to get them from him. "Thanks," I said, taking the small stack of envelopes.

"You're welcome. It's been quiet around here with Major in Rosemary Beach and Aida gone. I've got more time on my hands without having to listen to your momma telling me about the drama they've stirred up."

Chuckling, I went through the mail in my hands. "Yeah, Major kept things interesting. How's Uncle Chap doing with him working in the restaurant business?"

Dad shook his head. "Not proud of him, but I told him at least he's got a job. Don't think Chap's ever gonna get over the fact that his son slept with his wife. Don't know what he expected, marrying a woman four years older than his son."

I had to agree with him. "It's got to be hard being Chap's son, though." I never envied Major his father. Chapman Colt was a hard-ass to deal with. He was never my favorite uncle.

Dad grunted. "Probably so. Well, I got shit to do. I'll see you later. I reckon we're on our own for dinner, with the women out shopping."

Smiling, I nodded. "We'll make do."

He pulled away, and I went back to going through my mail. One envelope caught my eye, and I placed the other ones in my jacket pocket so I could open it. The simple white envelope had no return address. It was postmarked from Chicago and addressed to me.

I opened it and pulled out a thick set of folded papers. Something else fluttered to the ground. I opened the papers first, and my eyes immediately saw the words *Trust Fund* at the top. Just under it was Reese's full name.

I scanned the papers to see that Reese had a trust fund

worth ten million dollars, which she was entitled to the year she turned twenty-one. Confused, I continued reading, and Benedetto DeCarlo's name appeared. He'd done this. He had known where her mother was at one time, because he'd set up this trust fund. I wasn't sure how to tell Reese about this. Was this Benedetto's way of asking me for help in telling her?

I bent down to pick up the paper that had fallen out of the envelope. The small, square note looked familiar. I'd seen it before.

Turning it over, I saw that it simply said *For My Little Girl*.

Acknowledgments

First of all, I want to thank the Atria team. The brilliant Jhanteigh Kupihea. I couldn't ask for a better editor. She is always positive and working to make my books the best they can be. Thank you, Jhanteigh, for being awesome. Ariele Fredman for being not only brilliant with your ideas but listening to mine. Judith Curr for giving me and my books a chance. And everyone else at Atria that had a hand in getting this book to production. I love you all.

My agent, Jane Dystel. She is always there to help in any situation. I'm thankful that I have her on my side in this new and ever-changing world of publishing. Lauren Abramo, who handles my foreign rights. I couldn't begin to think of conquering that world without her.

The friends who listen to me and understand me the way no one else in my life can: Colleen Hoover and Jamie McGuire. You two have been with me from the beginning. Knowing I can call you both at any time when I need advice or just an ear is priceless.

My beta readers, Natasha Tomic and Autumn Hull. You both are brilliant and know exactly where to point out what is missing. Thank you so much for keeping up with my hectic schedule. Beta reading for someone who is always writing a book isn't an easy job.

Last but certainly not least: My family. Without their support I wouldn't be here. My husband, Keith, makes sure I have my coffee and the kids are all taken care of when I need to lock myself away and meet a deadline. My three kids are so understanding, although once I walk out of that writing cave they expect my full attention, and they get it. My parents, who have supported me all along. Even when I decided to write steamier stuff. My friends, who don't hate me because I can't spend time with them for weeks at a time because my writing is taking over. They are my ultimate support group, and I love them dearly.

My readers. I never expected to have so many of you. Thank you for reading my books. For loving them and telling others about them. Without you I wouldn't be here. It's that simple.